Secrets

Unearthed

Part Four

Chapter One

Here I was, back again, facing life or death decisions. Another package had been sent, but not in the way I had been expecting. Despite doing a thorough check for leaks, on multiple occasions information about what I got up to was still being fed to Cliff.

Now I had the choice of signing over my family's inheritance to a psychopath, who truly could never benefit from it considering he was a wanted felon, or let a cafe full of people plus anyone else who was in a twenty mile radius die.

Max had been returned to me in nearly one piece except from the fact he was now wearing a very dangerous accessory.

"I'm so sorry Abby, I never wanted this to happen. He was threatening my mum's life, I thought if I just did what he said I could try to save you after. I never wanted to hurt you in any way."

Max said, he was clearly emotional. He looked extremely worse for wear, his body was skinny and frail.

This speech of his felt like that of a dying man.

"When Cliff recaptured me he forced a doctor at gunpoint to save my life, I quickly realised there was no way of escaping that maniac. I woke up to my mum's dead body and a stitched up wound in my chest. Today I received instructions to follow, either I do as he says or I die."

He continued as he gestured to the bomb attached to his chest while speaking, it was due to go off in thirty minutes. His finger was on a dead man's switch and his other hand was bandaged up due to his missing finger.

"No one is blaming you Max, can't we let the people go at least?"

I pleaded with him.

"He's got a sniper on me, just like he did that day I kidnapped you for him. If I let anyone go he'll shoot which means we're all dead anyway."

I'd called the police through my watch and they'd been listening in this whole time. They were taking too long coming up with a plan.

I was out of options. I lunged forward, making sure there was no longer a clean shot available to the sniper. Pushing Max down to the ground I then laid on top of him. I had bet my life that the shooter would know he couldn't shoot me, without hesitation I switched the dead mans switch from Max's hand into mine.

I'm sure if he wasn't so weak or taken by surprise I'd normally never have tackled him to the ground so easily.

"Are you crazy?"

He asked. I looked around as I heard no gunshots fired.

"Now I control whether this bomb goes off or not. Do you hear me Cliff?"

I shouted loudly into the vest figuring he'd be listening in somehow.

"You can't get the inheritance if I'm dead now, can you!"

I said before standing up slowly.

Whilst helping Max to his feet I carefully blocked him from any shots that might still be aimed his way.

"Everyone you need to get out, quickly."

I said to the people still stuck in Rosie's Cafe. As soon as the people were out, a team of bomb experts were ushered in.

The police were sweeping the area for any signs of a shooter or anyone who could be working for Cliff. Sadly they still didn't believe that Cliff was out of prison.

They were able to remove the bomb and cover it with a dense metal dome. I was replaced by a bomb expert on the trigger and was removed from the area. They set off the bomb causing minimal damage to the Cafe. Although they would definitely need some renovations.

I couldn't help but feel sorry for Max as the medical team attended to his wounds. It's a wonder he hadn't died. It was like I was sitting next to a ghost who'd been brought back to life.

"How I felt about you was never a lie Abby."

His voice sounded broken, perhaps because I'd been staring at him he felt he owed me that.

"I'm not worried about that Max, I'm just glad you're alive. I'm so sorry about your mum."

I reassured him. His face fell as soon as he heard the word mum being mentioned.

To think this morning I'd been told to go pick up a package only to be nearly blown up yet again.

"You were brave back there, braver than me. If I'd told you the first day he contacted me or told your parents the truth when they confronted me and bribed me to leave… well maybe the outcome would have been different."

I looked up at him in surprise.

"I'm sorry? They bribed you?"

Max realised he'd revealed information I was previously unaware of and grimaced.

"Sorry, yeah, they accused me of leaking intel and paid me a large sum of money to break up with you and not come back. I took the money hoping I could get my mum out of harm's way. I thought I had for a bit. After I saw you that day at the Zoo he made contact again, but this time instead of just photos of her he actually had her hostage. I was supposed to trade you for her that day I got shot."

Max revealed.

I chose not to ask anymore questions. He'd been through enough already. Instead I took my clean bill of health and left him with the paramedics. Although this time his trip to the hospital would be guarded.

I was curious what the police were planning to do with him so I made a point to speak to them. The officer in charge assured me that he would be kept safe, after questioning they would be offering him a deal which would mean being put into witness protection.

I glanced back at Max offering him a sad smile as a condolence. This might very well be the last time I ever got to see his face again. As soon as I was free to go I rushed off home. My parents and Ralph hadn't been allowed onto the scene due to the danger and had been waiting for me back at the mansion.

Chapter Two

I arrived home to big sighs of relief and hugs from everyone, Simon was especially glad to see me. After reassuring everybody that I was fine, I requested to have a private talk with my dad about what Max had said.

Once alone in his office I confronted him about what I had learned.

"Dad, Max told me he was fired for being a leak. Why wouldn't you tell me something like that?"

I asked. I decided to keep the bit about bribery to myself.

My dad shifted uneasily in his chair which only led to me feeling less sure of what my parents were truly capable of.

"That's what we told him, yes. We couldn't exactly say the real reason we wanted him gone. Luckily for us he was a leak. So I guess we got away with it."

I knew he wasn't telling me the full story, I never believed the day would come that my father would lie to my face.

My mother's actions never surprised me but William has always been pure of heart in my eyes, until this moment.

"So you didn't know he was working for Cliff."

William shook his head sympathetically.

"Had we have known, you would have definitely been warned."

I truly wanted to believe him but Max had nothing left to gain from lying to me.

I knew that he was telling me his truth back in the ambulance.

"So you were just trying to get him to stop dating me by any means necessary then?"

I questioned him further.

"We may not have told him not to fraternise with our daughter but we couldn't have him working for us while doing so. He chose to leave his job, we didn't know he would break up with you because of it. Besides isn't it a good thing he left you considering who he was in bed with, no pun intended. Why do you care so much about the past anyway? You have Ralph now who you've assured me is the love of your life."

I decided to let it go for now and play along, I hadn't the energy to get to the bottom of this right now.

"No your right, it's just been a horrible day."

He stood up and gave me a hug. I excused myself and headed up to bed.

Before going to my room I went to check on Simon. He was playing on his phone with his bedside table lamp on.

"Busted."

I shouted, giving him a little fright. He laughed before turning his phone off.

"How do you always stay so cheery, even after going through hell and back?"

Simon asked.

My handsome teenager looked worried. I sat down next to him kissing him on his forehead.

"I tried being depressed and dwelling on all the wrong in my life. It got boring after a while, the day I met you changed my perspective on life. Each bad thing before you, led me *to* you so if more bad things are happening I can't wait to see what else I get for my trouble."

I answered him with a big grin. Simon chuckled in response.

"Doubt you can get better than me as a present."

He replied happily. I smiled at his witty response.

"Don't worry so much about me, I often get underestimated. I'm stronger than I look."

I said before I kissed and cuddled him goodnight and switched out his light.

He had grown so much, his fifteenth birthday was just around the corner. Soon he'd be so grown up he wouldn't need me anymore. Despite this thought trying to weigh me down I was still grateful to be able to call him my son.

Chapter Three

Ralph was waiting for me in my old room, he smiled at me as I climbed into bed. I was completely exhausted.

"Why do you look so happy?"

I asked as Ralph tried to stop smiling.

"It's not the time, you've had a rough day."

He replied. I sat back up in bed.

"It's okay, I could use some good news to cheer me up."

I answered. Ralph grabbed his laptop so he could show me a picture of a lady.

"Who is she and *why* is she supposed to cheer me up?"

I asked rather curtly. Ralph replied while still grinning.

"She's the perfect candidate, I want her to be our surrogate. She's available so just say the word and she will give us a baby."

He announced. I looked at Ralph feeling very confused.

"I almost died today and you want to discuss this, now?"

I asked, feeling a little annoyed. His face fell a little then his smile returned to his face.

"Let's face it, you're always in life threatening situations. Today was just a reminder of how short life can be, Abby I nearly lost you today at least give me this."

He replied. I grabbed my dressing gown before heading to a guest room slamming the door behind me.

That man was baby mad, it's all he could think about. I just needed a timeout, away from my *loving* husband. He hadn't even bothered to check if I needed emotional support or attention for what I'd been through.

Just as I was trying to get comfortable and sleep my phone started buzzing, without checking who it was I answered. I'd automatically assumed it was Ralph trying to ask me to come back to bed.

"I'm not interested in sleeping with you so just pleasure yourself and let me sleep."

I said. A familiar voice laughed sweetly in return.

"Well, you are attractive Miss Wilson, but I promise I just want to talk business with you."

It was Zuzanna, I felt so embarrassed.

"Ugh no, sorry I thought you were my husband, Ralph."

I said while grimacing.

"I was hoping you were free to meet as I'm flying to England tomorrow so I'll be available and in the area."

She replied. I was relieved to have been offered a distraction from all this surrogate talk.

Agreeing whole heartedly to meet her tomorrow I decided to throw caution to the wind and do what I wanted to do, for a change. Ralph could busy himself with baby planning and I could co-found a new charity.

I literally didn't have to be involved physically with any of the surrogate stuff considering my eggs had been frozen already and my womb wouldn't be the babies home.

After another hour of trying to sleep I gave up and returned to my own bed. Ralph was happily snoring away without a care in the world for my well being. It was almost as though as soon as I said 'I do' he no longer felt worried I was going to leave.

He'd stopped trying to make me happy, all he thought about was his needs. Even sex with him had changed. After some quick make up sex in the morning I agreed to take on his choice of surrogate.

Zuzanna and I met up and arranged all the details of what we wanted out of the charity and booked a date for the benefit. I had three months to pull off a groundbreaking event. Unfortunately we still hadn't come up with a name for our new charity.

Chapter Four

Despite all of the drama intruding on my life I had still found time to hold a benefit for my charity, it was a collaboration of the Angels Wings foundation and my No Means No organisation. Zuzanna Lambert was going to be the guest of honour.

We were joining the charities together to form a brand new movement which would be set up in the UK and one in America too. I needed the distraction, all Ralph wanted to talk about was the surrogate. A topic of conversation I was desperately trying to avoid.

We had met with a few ladies, agreeing on one in particular. Her name was Zoella, she was a beautiful middle aged, Spanish lady who had already had her own children. She loved pregnancies and needed cash, she had been a surrogate before with good reviews.

Zoella's hair was long and dark, with a figure that was very curvy but in an enticing way. For a lady in her forties she certainly didn't look any older than thirty years, I'm not sure if it was her olive skin that helped her look young or her glossy raven curls.

I just couldn't face any more talk about her impending pregnancy, it was bad enough that I would have to go to the appointment with them to insert the fertilised egg. I just wanted to bury my head in the sand and pretend none of it was happening.

I spent all week sorting out the arrangement for the benefit, after a very stressful five days I was ready for the arrival of my new benefactor. She was flying in a day early to meet me, we also had to come up with a name for the new charity.

At the airport I stood holding a sign saying 'Zuzanna Lambert', it brought me back to my first trip from America to the UK. It had been too many years since I had been the one being greeted by a sign with my surname on it, how far I had come since those awkward teen years.

Zuzanna came towards me, her look was distinctive with her Afro curls hanging down against her beautiful brown skin. She had such a luminous glow to her that would make the best of us jealous, next to her was another lady standing holding her hand.

"Zuzanna, amazing to see you again."

I said, greeting her happily.

She used her untethered hand to reach out for mine.

"Nice to see you again too Abigail, this is my fiancé Roselyn."

She replied. I shook both their hands before guiding them to the limousine. I couldn't help but admire their twin engagement rings.

"I like your matching rings."

I said, feeling a touch awkward around the loved up couple considering how 'unloved' up I was feeling.

"Thanks, Roselyn picked them out."

Zuzanna replied. The girls were smitten with each other.

If I had to guess I'd say that Zuzanna wore the trousers in the relationship, the clear breadwinner out of the two. She worried about business and her fiancé loved the glam lifestyle.

They were complete opposites yet seemed to be happier than most. Zuzanna wore a sensible pants suit and seemed to be all business, on the other hand Roselyn had luscious long blonde hair with fake everything.

She was beautiful in a very unique way, not your natural beauty but she had boobs twice the size of mine, tanned skin alongside a real 'beach babe' look.

"You have good taste Roselyn."

I said. She showed me her perfect white teeth as she thanked me for the compliment.

"Is your mother going to be here tomorrow?"

I asked eagerly. Zuzanna nodded.

"She's looking forward to meeting you, all I do is talk about you and our unidentified new charity. She actually helped me come up with a potential name."

I couldn't wait to meet the creator of 'Angels Wings'.

Anika Lambert was partly my inspiration behind my charity 'No Means No', I researched her life story and admired her greatly.

"The honour will be all mine, Anika is a hero in my books."

I said. Zuzanna also agreed with my comment.

"She is the whole reason I am here, I want to carry on her legacy... really make her proud."

Zuzanna said in reply. It was a touching sentiment.

When I was young I researched into loads of already existing charities, Angels Wings had to be my favourite out of them all. The backstory of Anika Lambert was inspiring, she had faced her fair share of cruelty at the hands of men in her life.

What I went through wasn't even a fraction of what she suffered, if she could stand tall so could I. We all sat down in a local Cafe, I showed them both my plans so far for our new charity.

"Have you had any luck choosing a name yet?"

Zuzanna asked me. I hadn't yet, I wanted to give credit to both names. So far I've come up with nothing good.

"Not yet, I wanted to incorporate both names somehow."

I replied. Zuzanna seemed to be against that idea.

"We already have Angels Wings which looks after young women trying to escape drugs and prostitution, No Means No protects women of all ages who are trying to escape domestic violence. This new charity is going to be ours, for the modern generation. I want it to focus on not just women but all young people who are struggling, things like suicidal thoughts and running away from home can cause such destruction to families. I want to be able to reach out to a wide variety of young people, those who struggle with their sexuality or a troubled home life. I thought maybe we could call it lifeline, what do you think?"

Zuzanna asked.

I had to admit I was a little surprised, yet her passion was infectious.

"Mum came up with lots of names reflecting the differences between us, I really want the name to unite us but none of the titles are ones I'm sold on, lifeline is my favourite but I wanted your input."

She said as she handed me a list of options. I too didn't like any of them enough but it did spark an idea of my own.

"This all sounds amazing. I do like lifeline as an option, but your speech has given me an idea. How about we call it 'Differences United'?"

Roselyn and Zuzanna looked at each other before wholeheartedly agreeing to use my chosen title.

It was so nice spending time with such a strong character. Zuzanna really wanted to help others, I think over the years I'd lost the fuel to my internal fire. This new charity was going to be the start of something amazing; I could just feel it in my bones.

I left the two love birds at their hotel, I had offered them a place at my parents mansion however they had wanted some 'alone time' in order to celebrate their recent engagement. I rang Simon in hopes that he would be free.

"Hi, Simon. Are you busy tonight?"

I asked him. He thankfully wasn't, I convinced him to come out for a meal with me. I hadn't had the chance to discuss Ralph's plans with the surrogate yet, I felt it was time I broached the subject with him.

Simon looked so grown up when we left the mansion, he had dressed up just for me. We left in style going to one of our favourite restaurants, we used to go there for every anniversary of the day I adopted him.

It seemed fitting that I do it on the day I talked about having another child, despite the baby not sharing Simon's DNA it would still be a part of his life.

Simon knew something was up, I guess I gave it away by my strange behaviour. He placed his hand on my shoulder.

"Mum, are you going to tell me what's going on?"

He asked. I smiled sheepishly, he knew me so well.

"Ralph and I have hired a surrogate, she is going to carry a child for us."

I replied. Simon was awfully quiet.

"Do you know what a surrogate is?"

I asked him. Simon raised his eyebrows at me

"Of course I do."

He replied. I often forgot how smart he had become.

"You only just married Ralph, straight after nearly breaking up with him. Do you really think it's the right time for a baby?"

Simon asked. He was right of course, but I couldn't let him know that his mum was simply a coward. I tried hard to defend myself.

"Most of our problems came from not being able to have kids, this way we can."

I replied. Simon shrugged in response.

"Whatever makes you happy, so long as this *will* make you happy."

He said. I smiled briefly before ordering our food.

Our conversation reverted back to normality. Simon had told me all about the things that I had missed in his life. He had actually met a girl, Zoe. She sounded nice... ish, they were both applying to go to sixth form.

Simon ended up going to the same school as I did, about eight years ago parents had applied for the girl and boy parts of the school to be merged.

It took them a few years of protesting but five years ago their plans had gone through to do construction on the school in order to join the two sections together.

Over the last couple of years girls and boys went to the school together successfully. Zoe had caught his eye over the last few months. They had been researching the benefits of sixth form together, she was well educated and from a good family.

On paper she was practically perfect so who was I to complain about their budding romance. I was probably just hesitant due to my bad memories of teenage romance. After much discussion and tasty food we finished up our dinner.

On my way out I noticed someone I recognised sitting on a dining table in the same restaurant, I could see Doctor Nicholas Romanos sitting with a lady and a young girl. The lady was not his wife yet they seemed cosy enough to be family.

His hand rested fondly on the lady's hand, the young girl looked just like him. I'm not sure why I was so outraged, I was a taken woman... Why should it bother me that he could potentially be a cheat? Maybe I was just jealous it wasn't me sitting across from him.

Try as I might, I could not get that image out of my head. I was offended to my core that he more than likely had a mistress and child behind his wife's back. This made me certain he had been trying to recruit me as another girl on the side.

I began running every conversation we had ever had through my head, maybe I had just imagined his flirtation. Could he have just been another person after more generous donations to his hospital. Although, he didn't seem the type.

Either way one thing was for certain, I would never talk to him ever again... I was certain of it. I just couldn't figure out why it bothered me so much. The next day I was up bright and early, not because I wanted to be but because it was the day of our surrogate's egg implantation.

I should have been pleased but none of it felt real, all I felt was a deadening numbness to my very being. Ralph held my hand so excitedly, he had wanted me to pray for success. I hadn't gone to church in a year at least, besides I didn't feel right asking for favours I might not even want.

I had prayed each time I fell pregnant that nothing would go wrong, it wasn't long after the last miscarriage that I stopped attending the church. Ralph had started going leading up to our wedding so that they would agree to marry us, I couldn't face it still now.

Instead I just let Ralph pray, pretending to agree with his request. I said amen but it was a hollow plea, I had wanted a child so badly that I had become desperate. Now I no longer wanted to mother a child, there had been too many unsuccessful attempts in the past.

I left the room shortly after the doctor had begun discussing all of the things that could go wrong, I needed to catch my breath. Zoella and Ralph came out shortly after, I stood by Ralph's side as we thanked Zoella.

She was going to stay with us until the pregnancy test could be done, not like our flat wasn't cramped enough as it was. I suggested that it might be better for me to stay at my Mums house, Ralph's stern look had made that decision for me.

I was trapped between Ralph and the woman who might end up carrying our child, everywhere I looked was a reminder of the fact that I couldn't just be honest. Deep down inside I knew there was a strong possibility that Zoella wouldn't be able to have my child.

I was starting to feel like I was destined to never have a child that shared my own DNA. I was okay with that, I just wish Ralph could be too. Hopefully after this attempt he would finally let it go.

Chapter Five

Listening to Ralph pander to Zoellas every need was too much for me to cope with. Thankfully I had a valid excuse to escape that day, my benefit was very much in need of my attention. Anika and Zuzanna were due to make an appearance along with some other distinguished guests, it was going to be a real 'America meets the UK' affair.

A fact that made me truly feel at home, I often visited America in the past whenever I had gotten the chance. Which lately had been fewer and far between. I had kept in touch with Patricia over the years, sort of. Truthfully I could have possibly made more of an effort when it came to contacting her.

She quite literally lived the American dream, she was a mum of two kids; a boy and a girl. They owned a dog who spent most of his days in the yard surrounded by a white picket fence. Patricia had married well, she was living an idyllic life.

We hadn't drifted apart on purpose, we just became extremely different people over time. It was so gradual that we took no notice of it until we were basically strangers. We took two opposite paths and had different views on life, love and family.

Patricia and I were 'friends' over social media, I still enjoyed seeing her status updates about baking pies and family picnics. I had led a very different life to her over the last ten years, the more married she became the less I felt a connection between the two of us.

My life may not be perfect but I was enjoying the journey, some days were just worse than others. Lately I'd felt that more of my days had been worse over being better.

I had dressed up in a lovely designer gown, my mother had demanded only the best for me to try on. Out of the three options I had chosen a sleek, sparkly, black dress draped in finery.

It had a slit up the side of my leg whilst also showing off some of my cleavage, I had to keep up with appearances you see. Everyone else would look stunning so I had to at least try to compete, with my hair and makeup now done I was ready to greet my audience.

I fanned out into the crowd greeting all the familiar faces, Leanne and her husband were going to be one of the first to say hello to me. Considering she was responsible for my current relationship she would be certainly wanting to gloat about her matchmaking success story.

She had clearly set her hopes on befriending me as part of a couple so that I could attend dinner parties. Although, since I tied the knot I had been too busy to accompany her to any of her events. Truth be told I had no close friends right now, aside from Ralph. Perhaps that's why I'd found it so hard to let him go, that and my cowardice.

I wasn't sure if it was because I hadn't made enough of an effort to keep people in my life or whether I just wasn't the long term friendship type of girl. I wanted to be, I longed to have that one person that I could share everything with and know I wouldn't be judged. That used to be Patricia.

I was tired of being a square peg bashed against that ever shrinking round hole. I wanted to belong somewhere... to someone… anyone. I was thoroughly engrossed in all of the attention from my guests, that was until the sight of Thomas hand in hand with his wife burned its way onto my eyeballs.

He strutted around the room holding his beautiful wife's hand with pride. Clearly she hadn't gotten my note that night. I was so embarrassed to be in the vicinity of the couple, so much so that I hastily turned around in order to escape, which only served to land me smack bang into Doctor Romanos, another man I was hoping to avoid.

His wife was also here at the party although she was currently on the opposite end of the room. As much as I was irritated upon seeing him, I had just tipped my drink all over his shirt. I hurriedly grabbed a cloth from one of my wait staff dabbing the soiled clothing now cloying to his muscular chest.

His hand touched mine as he insisted I stop, I quivered a little from his touch.

"It's fine, you can leave it. It is already ruined and I have a spare shirt in my friends car... Burt!"

He said, he signaled his friend to come over. He introduced us briefly before begging him to run and get his spare shirt from the car. Burt happily agreed and ran off.

"That was the guy I wanted to set you up with, although I doubt you want to be set up anymore considering you're a happily married woman now."

He said. I tensed up a bit. Reacting to my obvious discomfort he continued.

"You are *happily* married, aren't you Mrs Munson?"

He asked. Feeling annoyed again I decided to retaliate.

"I'm not sure what the sanctity of marriage means to the likes of you but I take my vows seriously. Excuse me, please."

I said. I could see his friend Burt returning with speed so I made myself scarce.

I had wanted to hide away however I knew I couldn't, my idol was waiting for an introduction. I saw Zuzanna with a magnificently beautiful older lady, she had to be in her late 60's yet looked great for her age.

Despite her age you could see her beauty as clear as day, she was the embodiment of an angel here on earth. With grey streaming all the way through her blonde long hair, she had placed it up in a high round bun.

Anika was adorned in a glamorous sparkling gold dress, she was even more impressive in person. I rushed over to greet her.

"Anika Lambert? It is so amazing to finally meet you. Your daughter and I are working together on 'Differences United'."

I announced proudly, extending my hand. Anika smiled kindly at me.

"I hear good things about you Abigail, judging by the event you're throwing I can see why."

She replied. I caught myself staring at her; I was in awe of this woman.

"Sorry, I don't mean to stare. I've read so much about your life. You were my main inspiration for starting up No Means No. I had so many things I wanted to ask you but now I'm just lost for words to be finally here in front of you."

I said, feeling giddy. Zuzanna shared a look of amusement with her mother before excusing herself.

The lovely Zuzanna bid me goodbye as she headed off into the sea of people wanting to talk with her. Once she had left her mother's side Anika continued.

"We all face challenges in life Abigail, it's how we overcome them that makes us who we are. You too have been through tough times, I recognise the look in your eye. A look mirrored in many of the women I have helped over the years, you were once a victim too."

She said. It was strange how she seemed to look into my soul.

"Yes I suppose that I was... long ago. How can you tell?"

I asked. Anika placed an arm around me.

"Perhaps more recently than that even, you are a strong woman. You need a good man by your side, all of us strong women do. I couldn't have gotten to where I am today without the love of a good man. You know you have found the right man when he lets you soar in the sky instead of keeping you weighed down to the ground. He will be your wings not your anchor."

She said. I laughed at her statement knowing that Ralph was definitely more of an anchor.

"I think I have a good guy, I married him recently. Although he is more of an anchor than anything else."

I replied honestly. Anika's kind eyes had pain deep within, I recognised it just as she did with me. She pulled me over to a quieter section of the room.

"I was your age when I got married, in my time marrying a black man was frowned upon to say the least. We made it, against all odds. You just have to find someone worth fighting for. I have written a book about my life, 'Siostra'. It means sister in polish. You should read it. Not all abuse is physical or obvious, sometimes ignorance can be just as damaging. Know your worth, claim what you deserve."

She said kindly. I eagerly wrote down the name on a piece of paper lying around, we had sign up sheets and pens on a table beside us.

"I can't wait to read it, I researched all about your life and how you came from nothing. You really turned your life around and became someone great."

I said. Anika chuckled heartily.

"I had a lot of hard decisions to make before I became 'great' as you put it. I made mistakes, a lot of them. If your husband isn't making you happy then you should do something about that, if it's meant to be then it works even in the hard times... especially in the hard times. That is the true test of a man's love. **You should both be willing to lay your life down for the other, at the same time you should never try to take control of one another. You have to love your partner just as they are, not who they could be."**

With that piece of wisdom imparted she left my side to go back to be with her daughter. Her words rang in my mind, none of what she was saying could be said for my relationship with Ralph.

Not that I planned to divorce him just because I was unhappy, he hadn't done anything wrong to me yet stayed with me despite all I had put him through. I owed him.

It was now time for me to make my announcement. I got up on stage in front of a room full of faces staring up at me. Some were known to me while others were brand new, it was just like being back on that pulpit giving my late grandmother's eulogy on the day of her funeral.

I had that same pit of emptiness brewing inside of my stomach, pushing aside those feelings I introduced Zuzanna so that she could talk about our new charity. I hurriedly left the stage shortly after.

The rest of the night flew past, with applause and donations galore I left without any goodbyes. I had gotten my mother to agree to take over in my place, she was more than capable of making sure everyone got a goody bag as they left.

I would always give away something special with leaflets containing important information, this year we were handing out small bottles of a popular perfume. A male version and a female version were available to whoever wanted one, I normally loved handing out the gifts yet tonight I had just wanted to escape.

Not that home was much of an escape for me, thankfully Ralph and Zoella were fast asleep when I got home. Zoella hadn't been feeling well so Ralph chose to stay home in case it was anything serious.

I was just happy to get a night off from him. Yet I was still a little annoyed that he hadn't chosen to be by my side tonight. Thinking back, I should have questioned his motives a bit more. I had just stopped caring altogether... about everything.

Chapter Six

I didn't even attempt to look at my phone last night, I woke up with so many missed text messages and phone calls. My mother was demanding my presence at work today. I had been taking a back seat lately, considering all the work I had to do to bring my new charity to life.

There was one text that I hadn't been expecting, Nicholas had messaged me asking if we could talk. I immediately deleted his text, I had no interest in being a part of another affair or being his confidant about his current affair. I had already learnt the hard way that married men never leave their wives, nor should they.

If I ever caught Ralph cheating I'm not sure what I'd do, hypocritical as it may be I'm not sure I could forgive him the way he had forgiven me. I wasn't going to let myself fall for another married guy, I certainly couldn't allow him to fill my head with lies. Besides, I was with Ralph, wasn't I?

I snuck out of the flat before he stirred, Zoella was fast asleep in the guest room just as she had been last night. As I drove into work I thought about blocking the doctors number, for some unknown reason I hadn't done it yet.

What was I still holding on to? It was almost as if it had become comforting to know he could have been an option. However, he was clearly another Thomas; like I needed another pain in my ass. Considering his job role I decided not to be petty, in case he ever did contact me in a professional manner.

Best not to burn bridges over his actions, especially considering I wasn't directly affected by them. Taking a large breath in, I released it with frustration. I just wanted to wish him out of existence. Terrible as that may seem I just didn't need him in my thoughts anymore.

Mum was very much overworked, as I got into her office I could see the stacks of paperwork surrounding her.

"Finally, I can't run this place alone forever you know!"

She announced angrily. I mocked her stress face before scooping up a large tower of files and taking them into my office.

Back to normality, it felt good to get back to my daily routine. By the end of the day I had the office purring like a baby kitten, there was a dull hum of happy workers whilst everything ran smoothly again.

Deidre came knocking at my office door, she had decided to go home early for once. Simon made his own way home these days so at least I didn't have to worry about pick up and drop offs anymore.

Although, part of me missed him needing me for school runs.

"Soon I'm going to have to retire and leave this company in your hands, you do a much better job running the place than I do. My only issue is that you aren't here as often as you should be."

She said. I glanced up for a moment before returning to work.

"You're not that old yet Mum, besides we still need you around here. You can be my secretary after I take over."

I said jokingly. My mother came over to kiss me on top of my head before attempting to leave.

"You couldn't afford me sweetheart, the time is coming sooner or later. Whether you like it or not I am going to retire one of these days. As much as I need you, they need you too Abigail."

She smiled wryly as she escaped the office, anyone that tried to speak to her on her way out got redirected to my office. I could tell it was going to be a late one. Not that I minded, time away from Ralph and the baby maker was very much what I needed.

I threw myself into work, I barely saw Ralph or Zoella. She had been unsuccessful the first time, Ralph kept harassing me to try again however I kept fobbing him off. It was bad enough going through the miscarriage myself, I had convinced myself that my womb was the problem.

It happened again in someone else's womb, it had to be my eggs. When they were frozen, the doctor at the time had reassured me that my eggs were perfectly healthy and would be a strong candidate from IVF.

Despite my protests about trying again Zoella was still living with us. Ralph was adamant that she was going nowhere as he was determined to change my mind. I however, knew that I wouldn't be budging. He either accepts my decision or I guess we were over.

One night at the office I had decided to go home early, I thought I could surprise Ralph. I hadn't exactly been the best wife lately, I couldn't remember the last time we had sex. I also wanted to put this baby issue to bed and get Zoella out of our flat.

I left my mum in charge of the office so that I could go home and whisk him out for the evening. As I entered our tiny flat, noises could be heard. I saw half an open bottle of wine on the coffee table, the lights were set to dim.

To be honest my first thought had gone to the fact that Ralph was watching porn, so in order to embarrass him I snuck into the room. What I saw was not at all what I had expected, Ralph was not jerking off alone in front of the TV screen as I had predicted.

Actually, Ralph was completely naked thrusting himself into Zoella, she looked great considering how many kids she had given birth to. I was frozen in shock as I watched my husband dipping his penis in and out of our surrogate, he hadn't been that energetic with me in quite some time.

She had her bottom poised upwards and her face flat on the bed, I could literally see everything as it was happening. Almost as if it were in slow motion, I witnessed the tip of his penis dip in and out of her vagina as if he were enjoying himself so much he didn't want it to end. Grabbing a hold of her breasts he teased her nipples.

"Yeah baby, let daddy make a baby inside you."

Ralph said. He began banging her harder and harder.

"Yes daddy, give me a baby."

She shouted.

You would think I would have had the sense to leave the room yet I stood there motionless, he pressed her body down on the bed as he lay down on top of her, he pushed on the back of her head as he spoke again.

"I'm cuming."

He exclaimed. Zoella replied after she gave him a moment to ejaculate.

"You wanna do it again?"

She asked.

It was when they attempted to change positions that they spotted me still staring in disbelief, his hard penis soon went limp as he realised what was happening. I headed straight to the wardrobe and started packing my things, I ignored the pleas of Ralph as his lover ran out of the room.

He was busy trying to convince me that he was just having sex with her in order to make her pregnant, of course his infidelity was just for us. The icing on the cake was when he blamed the fact that I refused to try again using Zoella as our surrogate.

Of course it was my fault, me not wanting to have a baby apparently was reason enough to cheat. Every moment of my life since meeting Ralph flashed before my eyes. Never in all my wildest dreams had I considered this being a thing that could happen.

Once I had packed my stuff I headed straight to the front door, I placed the album he had made for me as a gift on the coffee table. I had no use for that in my life anymore.

Ralph clung onto my arm begging me to stay.

"You're my wife Abby you aren't going anywhere."

Ralph announced as he blocked my way out.

"You cheated on me more than once and I forgave you. You can't leave just because of this! I won't allow it."

He said.

All of my pent up rage was seeping out of me. I slammed my suitcases down.

"Get out of my way Ralph! You can't stop me."

I said angrily. He simpered as he moved aside.

"You see, the main tether holding me to you was the fact that you would never hurt me. Despite all I had put you through, you stayed. I felt I owed you. Now you have shown what you're really capable of. You were the anchor weighing me down but now I'm free to fly."

I said as tears streamed down my face.

"Please don't do this Abby, we can work this out. I fucked up but you can forgive me, find it in yourself to forgive me."

He pleaded.

"That's the thing Ralph, I'm not hurt by your actions. At least not for the reasons I should be. I stood there watching you fuck that whore in there yet I felt nothing. It suddenly became clear to me, I don't love you Ralph. I just don't. I forgive you but I don't want to be your wife. I want to be free. The only thing that hurts is the fact that having a baby was more important than being faithful. Please Ralph, let me go... I'm drowning. You used to be my

life jacket but now you're pulling me under water. I want a divorce."

I said. With sorrow in his eyes he agreed to let me leave but begged me to reconsider.

There was no way I would stay with him. I should have left him years ago, I had let fear dictate my fate. In a way, I was glad that I had witnessed that image, I had placed Ralph on a pedestal thinking he could do no wrong. I guess everyone could become a cheat under the right circumstances, even the good guys.

In that moment I decided to be more open minded when it came to married people and their problems. I text Nicholas, I replied to his text even though it was from months ago. I sent a message saying 'Let's talk.'

I also decided to forgive myself, it wasn't easy always doing the right thing. I should have left Ralph for the sake of both of us, if I had let him go he could have had a kid by now with someone else and I could have potentially found someone that I actually wanted to be with.

Instead I had let our relationship grow into this sick and twisted mess, it was a dying animal that had to be put down yet I let it go on despite the pain we were both in. Through mistakes we become who we are meant to be, this mistake was the best thing that could have happened to me.

I arrived home to see my parents sitting in their favourite chairs in the green room, my dad immediately noticed something was up. After I explained what I had just witnessed, my dad had threatened to go kick his ass. I laughed through the tears at his eagerness to beat up Ralph.

I refused to let him do anything to Ralph.

"Dad it's okay. I cheated on him too, a long time ago. That's why we split up the first time. I didn't love him the way I should have. In a way I'm glad it's over, finally."

I said. They both hugged me, I tried not to be sad but I had just lost my best friend. Truth be told he was lost long ago, I was just unwilling to admit it and move on.

I was short on friends lately, losing Ralph was a tough pill to swallow. When Simon woke up I let him know that we were over, so was the idea of me having another child. He hugged me which I enjoyed, being a teenager he didn't often offer me hugs anymore.

I would have clung onto him for hours if he had let me, of course the moment was spoiled. My phone had been ringing a lot today, I hadn't bothered to answer it considering all that had happened in the last twenty-four hours. The house phone had rung this time, the hospital was the one trying to get a hold of me.

I headed off to speak with the unknown person calling from the hospital, I had no clue why they would be calling. A voice came through the phone, one I hadn't expected.

"Mrs Munson, is that you? It's Doctor Romanos here."

He said.

"It's Miss Wilson actually, but yes. How can I help you."

I replied.

"Sorry to hear that. I am calling in a professional capacity. It's of a sensitive nature, would you be able to come in today?"

He asked. There was no arrogance in his voice, just sincerity.

I agreed to meet him in the office, what choice did I have? I would have to find out one way or another what the 'sensitive' subject he couldn't discuss over the phone was.

I found myself searching rapidly through my clothing so that I could find something to wear. I shouldn't be adjusting my appearance for the married doctor but nevertheless here I was deciding on which outfit made me look best.

After deciding on my favourite jeans, I quickly picked a top before grabbing my coat. That would have to do, what did it matter what I looked like anyway. I didn't want to give him the wrong impression of me.

Chapter Seven

I arrived at the hospital as quick as I could, I applied makeup mostly just to hide the fact I had been crying. It wasn't long before I'd reached his office.

Nicholas was looking particularly irresistible in his work attire, what can I say? I clearly became drawn to men in white jackets, not that Ralph and Nicholas had anything else in common.

Except for maybe being cheats, I was beginning to think every man had that in common. I barged into his office even though he was deep in conversation over the phone.

" I got to go now, my patient is here. Talk soon. Uh, hello Abigail. I wasn't expecting you so soon."

He said, looking rather flustered as he hung up the phone.

"Sorry, was I interrupting a private call. You told me to come to your office... so that's what I did."

I replied.

"Please sit down, I'd like to discuss something with you."

He said.

There was a difference in his demeanour. Whatever the reason for it, I decided that I should be professional with my doctor. I sat down respectfully awaiting the impending news to fall upon me, I hadn't quite been prepared for what he had to say.

"I did try to get a hold of you a few months ago as I wanted to ask you a few questions. I was asked to look into your inability to get pregnant, your most recent attempt to have a baby with your surrogate stirred up concern. I was sent your medical file, something about it was bothering me. I don't normally get Involved In these cases but you're Mr Munson had been insistent. He came in to see me just after your benefit. When your surrogate failed to get pregnant I started looking into your case. When nothing was making sense I had your eggs tested."

He said. I was very confused by what he was trying to say to me.

"I discovered that there are signs of tampering with your frozen eggs, they have been rendered useless due to a drastic drop in temperature. I've checked the video for the time and date that this happened. There is evidence of someone opening your eggs and swapping out the samples of sperm we had."

He continued. He showed me the video footage. I was in a state of shock. Matthew was on camera, the time and date matched when I was first starting IVF treatments with Ralph years ago.

Pulling back I felt as though I might throw up.

"So what does this mean, moving forward?"

I asked trying to avoid airing my dirty laundry in front of Nicholas.

"Your eggs are no longer viable for use, and sadly due to the damage to your reproductive system you won't be able to have children."

He said before reaching for a cheque book.

On one hand I was relieved to know why I hadn't been able to get pregnant but on the other side of it I was infused with anger over the fact Matthew had been the final nail in the coffin of my dreams of having a baby.

"The hospital would like to compensate you for this happening on our watch. Something like this should never have happened."

Nicholas said. He handed me a large cheque but I refused to accept it.

"I don't want your money but I do need you to do something for me. It possibly will go against your doctor's oath but you owe me."

I replied. I needed his help to prove Cliff wasn't behind bars. He was going to help whether he liked it or not.

"Look I want to help, what would you have me do?"

He replied.

"There is a man in prison, I need you to prove he isn't who he claims to be. Do that and I won't sue the hospital."

I said with a firm expression. He looked deeply into my eyes.

"I'm not sure how I can make that happen but I agree to your terms."

He said. I couldn't help but be curious as to why he was so interested in helping me.

"Why?"

I asked him. Nicholas smiled sadly.

"My marriage wasn't strong enough to endure the fact I couldn't have kids, I don't want to be presumptuous in thinking your marriage is struggling for the same reason. Either way I know a little of what you're going through."

He replied.

His honest answer surprised me. I looked at his hand and saw that he wasn't wearing his ring, then I started to realise I possibly had him all wrong.

"Well I don't suppose your wife cheated on you but I guess you could say not being able to have kids was one of the reasons I left my husband. Could have also been his infidelity or mine. I honestly can't tell you exactly what went wrong."

I spoke with a broken voice as I tried hard to keep in the tears. He rested his hand on mine.

"My wife cheated on me, although I thought about doing it too I just couldn't do it. We saw a counsellor but nothing helped. Sometimes it's just not meant to be."

He pulled his hand away before clearing his throat.

"If you could test the sperm too, I think you will find that the man in the video footage was a patient of yours. His sperm will be in the vials. You can report it to the police, if I do they won't believe me. They are likely to take it seriously if it comes from you."

I told him. I stood up trying to regain my composure.

"Trust me it's a blessing I didn't get pregnant if Ralph was going to be the father."

I said. Feeling like we had possibly crossed over the patient doctor relationship enough for today I made an excuse and left the room.

I guess I shouldn't have assumed Nicholas was the same as Thomas. Still I wasn't ready to be in any relationship with a man, friendship or otherwise. Seeing Matthews face again was a little more than I could handle right now.

Needing some much needed space I left the hospital and found myself driving around aimlessly. I ended up parked outside of the firehouse. I could see Thomas getting ready to go out in his fire engine.

He looked over to where I was parked, before he had the chance to come over to speak with me I got the hell out of there. I just wanted to see his face but no good could ever come from speaking to him again.

Chapter Eight

Without saying a word to my parents about my visit to Dr Romanos I continued as though nothing was out of place. I couldn't wait for the DNA results to come my way but I would have to be patient. I had no idea how Nicholas would even acquire what he needed to help prove I wasn't crazy.

As for the sperm, he had already checked and confirmed that I was accurate in my assumption; Matthew had been a match. I'd given him specifics about who in prison I needed to be checked and where he could find his original DNA samples.

Now it was just a waiting game. I was completely caught off guard when I arrived home; Ralph had decided to stop by and see me despite the fact we weren't currently on speaking terms.

I half expected him to be a broken man, on his knees begging for me to take him back but instead he looked happy to see me.

"Hi Ralph, can I help you?"

I asked, feeling a little uneasy over his presence.

"It's nice to see you too Abigail."

He replied. He handed me an envelope.

"If you don't mind I'd like to get this over with so I can get out of here unscathed."

He said. I looked at the paperwork inside, he had filed for an annulment.

"I'll have to get my lawyer to look this over."

I said in reply.

"Sure. But I'm not asking for anything other than the dissolution of our marriage."

He said. I nodded, trying hard not to give away any indication that I was hurt by his request.

Ralph left the mansion without even looking back, I immediately went to see my dad to show him the paperwork.

"I'll give it to the lawyer Abby but if you want my opinion it would be a get out of jail free card. You signed no prenuptial agreement and he would be entitled to half of your charity and everything else that is currently yours. Although you could take half of his restaurant chain but you're worth more than he is."

William said.

"But, he's reasons for an annulment are based on lies. Isn't that fraud?"

I asked.

"Abby, unless you have video recordings of what goes on in the bedroom there is no way of proving it's a lie. If you both agree the marriage was never consummated, than who is going to call you out and say you're lying?"

He replied. I was a little annoyed that William was so comfortable with this level of dishonesty.

"Trust me, a divorce will be far messier. Just give the man what he wants and move on with your life."

He said, finally. Not knowing what to say to him I left without replying. Instead I kept my head down and focused on work.

The next day the office was in chaos yet again, anytime I left things seemed to fall apart. I had lost interest in running this place a long time ago, I hadn't the heart to tell my mum that the company she had poured her adult life into wasn't for me.

To be fair I didn't know what I loved doing aside from the charity work, I had wanted to get into medicine when I was younger. Trying many different hobbies over the years, the only thing I'd been interested in was being a mother to Simon. That was a job I thrived at, now he was getting older he needed me less and less.

Feeling a little lost when it came to my career choices, or just choices in general I wasn't willing to rock the boat and quit now. Not after all my parents had done for me over the years, I was much safer staying where I was. Although saying that, my choice to stay with Ralph had come from the same reasoning and look how that had gone.

I arrived just in time to catch my mother losing her temper with our suppliers, she was deep in conversation over the phone trying to convince them that they should be grateful we even gave them a contract in the first place.

As soon as she noticed me standing there, Deidre quickly ended the call.

"What time do you call this Abigail? I have been 'run' off my feet all day trying to fix this ultimate cock up from our suppliers."

My mother said. She had clearly reached her limit for the day.

"I had a meeting with our lawyer. I'm here now, go home and put your feet up. I'll stay and sort this out, alright?"

I replied. Mum strongly agreed with me that she needed to relax so she took me up on my offer, by the time I had a chance to turn around she was gone.

I must have stayed at work until 'gone midnight', I sent the workers home early. With me alone in the office I got far more done than being distracted by continuous questions.

After hours, swimming in the sea of paperwork, I was finally able to come up for air around one o'clock in the morning. I saw some missed calls on my phone from Nicholas, Ralph and Simon.

I text Simon apologising for being late home, I offered my apology in the form of breakfast 'on me' as a way of making it up to him. I worked myself into a coma, before I even realised it I had quite literally fallen asleep at my desk.

The sun was the one to rudely interrupt my sleep, not that I didn't need the wake up call. I was having a strange dream involving Nicholas and Ralph, sadly there was no sex involved.

They were having a baking contest and I was the judge, I honestly preferred Nicholas's exotic flan yet I chose Ralph's bland rice pudding instead. I'm sure a therapist would have had a field day over dissecting all the hidden meanings behind it, not that I was willing to part from my time and money to hear their assessment.

After spending a minute in the bathroom fixing my face, I headed out, locking up the office behind me. I hurried in order to make it in time for breakfast with Simon, he had requested that we meet at our favourite cafe.

By the time I reached Rosie's Cafe I was starting to feel the consequences of sleeping at my desk, there was definitely a crick in my neck developing. Simon was waiting for me outside.

"Mum, you look like crap. Are you sleeping at your office now?"

He asked. I agreed that I had. I was looking forward to catching up with Simon, it was the best part of my day.

I always felt a little unsettled on the days that I didn't see him, the older he got the more days I went without seeing him. He had wanted to talk to me about something important, that's why he had been ringing me last night. After we had grabbed a seat at the cafe I queried him.

"What did you want to talk to me about?"

I asked. Simon blushed a little before broaching the subject.

"Well, it's my sixteenth birthday soon. Zoe and I are getting on really well, I asked her to be my girlfriend last week."

He announced. Ignoring the shock on my face he carried on.

"I wanted you to help me arrange a romantic night at a hotel, for my birthday. I want Zoe to be my first... you know."

He revealed. After allowing the shock to fade, I tried to process what he had just told me.

My son wanted to have sex for the first time. On one side of the matter I was so happy that he trusted me enough to come to me, on the other hand it was a painful reminder of the fact he was growing up so fast. I smiled briefly before asking the hard question.

"Do you love her?"

He asked. Simon shrugged.

"She's like the hottest girl in school, what's not to love?"

He replied. I bit my tongue slightly, he was just a kid after all.

Perhaps I should have phrased my question better, I meant was he in love with the girl. Either way I had his answer, now it was my job to let him live his life.

"If you're sure that this is what you want to do, I'm all for helping you pull it off. Please make sure she is sixteen before you do anything like that with her. Is she a virgin too?"

I asked. Simon laughed at me.

"She's almost seventeen, she got held back a year and she's no virgin. We've already done stuff, I just wanna go all the way in style. I want to remember my first time for all the right reasons."

He answered. I could never refuse that boy anything that he wanted, as much as I'd prefer he wait for love. I knew that I was in no position to dish out demands.

I hadn't exactly chosen a good guy for my first go at making love, so I decided to keep my opinions to myself.

"Well it looks like you've thought things through, you're growing up so fast. Can't you just stay young forever?"

I asked. He laughed off my very real request, I can't believe he was now the same age that I was when I was dating his father.

Chapter Nine

Our breakfast was brief but I can't say I wasn't pleased to finally make it home, the one thing I was in desperate need of was a nice hot soak in the tub.

It was a Sunday which meant no work today, I intended on ignoring the world and having a much needed 'me' day. I sat in that bath sipping wine until half the bottle had gone and the water had become tepid.

Try as I might I could not get Nicholas out of my mind, I checked my phone for any calls or texts but there were no new ones. After finally giving up on my bath I decided on taking a nap, mostly because I hadn't eaten and the wine had gone straight to my head.

Even though I had slept for over an hour I still had no message or call from the doctor. I could call him, I just thought he would have tried to reach me again by now. I decided to text him instead.

I wrote a message apologising for missing his call and asking if he'd had any luck on his quest. It wasn't long before I saw the phone ringing, it was Nicholas.

"Hello, Miss Abigail Wilson speaking."

I said.

"Hello, I was trying to reach you last night as I managed to come up with a viable plan. I'm actually at the prison now so I'll let you know how it all goes."

He replied before ending the call. With little else to do I decided to browse through social media to see what everyone else was up to.

I was surprised to see that I had received a friend request from Doctor Romanos. Feeling curious I went straight onto his information page, looking at his details. He's relationship status said it's complicated which didn't bode well for me. Nor did the fact that the beautiful lady I had seen him eating with in the restaurant was all over his profile page.

She had the same surname, Olivia Romanos. Could it be he had already remarried? Perhaps she was his sister. Her pictures were stunning, even better than how she looked in person. One thing stood out the most, next to her relationship status read married.

It seemed odd that their statuses didn't match each other's, if they were together I'm sure they would. Who knows what his story was but for now I just accepted his request and got on with my day.

Patricia's profile was the next one I clicked on. She, of course, was enjoying herself immensely. Her perfect family photo had just been posted, enjoying their BBQ.

With my mood plunging I decided to bite the bullet and call Ralph. It was time to finalise the end of my marriage. I invited him over so I could give him the signed paperwork in person.

In no time at all he had arrived to collect it.

"I'm glad you finally came to your senses."

He announced as he clasped hold of the envelope.

"I don't like signing a fraudulent document Ralph but you deserve to be happy and move on without having to go through a messy divorce."

I replied.

"Zoella is pregnant, we want to get married before the baby comes so you can understand why I can't wait through a year of separation. I appreciate you doing this for me."

Ralph said. I realised in that moment that as much as he possibly loved me at one point, having a baby had meant so much more to him.

"I doubt I'm invited to the wedding but feel free to send me your gift list and I'll be sure to get you something."

I said politely. Ralph kissed me on the cheek unexpectedly.

"I'm sorry it had to end this way,"

He said before leaving me alone with my thoughts.

Much later into the evening Nicholas rang me again.

"So, how did it go?"

I asked him eagerly.

"I have acquired the DNA samples I need so all I have to do now is bring it to the hospital and I'll let you know as soon as I have the results."

He replied. I paused for a moment.

"Would you like to go out for dinner?"

I asked. I was surprised myself that I had said it. Nicholas hesitated before answering.

"Like a date?"

He asked. Feeling nervous I decided to play it off as a friendly offer.

"Ah no, just to thank you for your help."

I replied.

"Oh, I see. I guess that would be okay. Although I did owe you a favour. So we could just call it even."

He said. I was definitely getting the vibe he wasn't available.

"Sure. Well please let me know when you get the results."

I replied before quickly hanging up.

Feeling completely sorry for myself I went searching through Patricia's profile page before drinking the rest of the wine and passing out. I woke up feeling terrible so I decided to take a sick day.

Deidre let me off, considering I had just ended my marriage. I slept in for most of the day; feeling sorry for myself had made me sleepy. That and the hangover I was featuring.

I hadn't realised but I'd left my phone open the entire night. My phone chimed through saying I had a chat window open. Thinking I was online Nicholas had sent a message saying 'hello'. I replied in kind. Our conversation went as follows:

Nicholas: Hello

Me: Hi

Nicholas: I'm sorry about last night. I'd actually love to go for dinner sometime, if the offer still stands.

Me: Is it a date?

Nicholas: Touché

Me: I'd love to, but I just want to put something out there. Although I've just dissolved my marriage, I don't want to be stepping on any toes. I hope you don't have anyone in your life who would have an issue with our dinner.

Nicholas: I guess I was right about Ralph after all. I think Burt is still single... I could invite him to join us if you prefer. I'm currently unattached so we wouldn't be upsetting anyone, besides it's just dinner.

Me: I thought it was 'complicated', or so I read. As far as Burt goes I think I have my eye on someone else.

Nicholas: 'It's complicated' is just one step away from being single. But I might have a cure for that wandering eye of yours.

Me: So long as you leave your arrogant bedside manner behind, I'm sure dinner will be quite enjoyable.

Nicholas: I could say the same about your snappy side, but I still want to eat with you. Shall we say tomorrow at eight? I may have the results by then.

Me: I guess, we could say... it's a date?

Nicholas: It's a date.

With that we both signed off. I wasn't a hundred percent certain what I had just signed up for, but I was looking forward to seeing how the night went.

Chapter Ten

    I was feeling much better today. Work was a breeze; I couldn't wait until dinner with Nicholas. I quickly got dressed and ready to leave. Nicholas was waiting at the restaurant for me.

"You look nice, Mum. Have you got a hot date?"

Simon asked. I laughed coyly.

"Actually, I'm not sure if it's a date or not, he is hot though."

I answered. Winking at a curious Simon I left the mansion in a hurry.

I was worried that if I thought for too long I'd end up backing out of the date, due to nerves. I figured if I kept busy then I wouldn't have time to change my mind. It was working, until I reached the restaurant. I was now stood, staring gormlessly through the glass window, all those happy couples made me feel uneasy. How come everyone else seemed to find a blissful love companion?

I forced in a deep breath, as I breathed it out steadily I walked up to the guy in charge of the bookings. Before I had the chance to state my name Nicholas had already sent for me, he must have seen me coming in. I was running a bit late.

They led me to where he was sitting, as I came closer I saw Olivia from his profile page sitting next to him. All I could think was that I hoped it wasn't one of those threesome situations. I hadn't got involved with any crazy 'sexcapades' in my twenties, I certainly didn't plan on trying it out now.

Hesitantly I sat down at the table with them, feeling a little ambushed.

"Abigail, this is Olivia. She is my sister in law."

He announced. I felt beyond awkward as I smiled in her direction, perhaps I shouldn't have dressed up for the occasion after all. Olivia grinned at me.

"Nicholas has told me so much about you, I'm so glad that we can finally meet."

She replied. I had no words that I could say out loud whilst in polite company.

"I hope you don't mind me crashing your date, it's just that I've been struggling with the lonely nights lately."

Olivia said. She seemed genuinely sad.

"Oh don't worry it's just a date for friends, isn't that right Doctor."

I replied. Nicholas blushed a little.

"You can call me Nicholas, Abby. I'm sorry for all the awkwardness on my part. I figured as a threesome we could keep it casual."

He said. Olivia laughed out loud realising what was going on, before even I had figured it out.

"It all makes sense now, Nick you like this woman so much that you need me here as a buffer."

She said quietly to him. His cheeks flushed red before he excused himself from the table.

"I'll go talk to him."

Said Olivia. I felt a tad awkward being alone on the table so I ordered a bottle of wine in their absence.

I drank a whole glass before they rejoined me.

"I have to go now, my husband is in hospital at the moment. I'm going to go see him then head home. I'll see you back at the house Nick."

Olivia announced before leaving. Nicholas quickly sat back down.

"Your brother is in hospital?"

I asked, trying to ease the tension.

"Ah yes, stubborn mule, he refused to let anyone else operate on him. He said it had to be me."

He replied, laughing lightly.

"I hope he's alright?"

I asked.

"He was injured in a car accident, I'll spare you the details but he ended up in need of a serious operation. He will make a full recovery."

Nicholas answered.

Feeling utterly mortified by the way I had just assumed the worst of Doctor Romanos, I immediately apologised for jumping to conclusions about him.

"I feel stupid now, but I had initially thought she was your mistress, her kid looks just like you."

I said. Nicholas looked at me oddly. Realising he didn't know, I revealed that I had seen them in a restaurant together some time ago.

"I can see how you might jump to that conclusion. My wife and I separated for a year but are now very much divorced. She cheated on me with a mutual friend of ours actually. A certain firefighter who visited you in hospital. They met that day actually."

Nicholas replied. I suddenly realised that I unwittingly had partly helped end his marriage.

"Oh God, I'm so sorry."

I said, choosing not to bring up the fact I too had joined in an affair with that same man.

"Not your fault. But it's all still a bit fresh, I do find you attractive and want to pursue things with you but we may have to take things slowly."

He replied. I smiled before resting my hand on his.

**"I literally dissolved my marriage yesterday. I don't think
I could do anything fast either right now."**

I replied. We spent the night discussing a wide array of
topics. I asked all about his brother and Olivia.

The woman seemed to have it all, her parents were
born in italy but she had lived here her whole life. Her
husband was a dentist which was clear from her perfect white
veneers, showing every time she opened her mouth.

I didn't know what her husband looked like, all I knew
was that he was one lucky man. The turquoise dress that she
wore, showing off her cleavage, long legs and tiny waist was
enough to give anyone a complex about their own figure.

**"I'm sorry that I invited Olivia along, I was just
nervous to be around you in this setting."**

Nicholas said.

**"It's okay. Forget about it. Although I hope you
don't mind me asking, why can't you have kids?"**

I asked. He was a little surprised by my question. After realising he already knew why I couldn't he then proceeded to answer.

"The medical term for it is Hypogonadism. I have a low level of testosterone in my body caused by a tumour which has now been removed. Thankfully being a doctor, working most days in a hospital, it was caught early."

He answered. I shared a sympathetic look with him. More than likely that was why he became so curious about my inability to conceive a child.

I felt I should share an embarrassing truth to make us even. My cheeks grew slightly pink even before I began speaking.

"I walked in on my now ex fiancé having sex with our surrogate, she's now pregnant. Which of course means our marriage needed to be annulled quickly so he can marry her. That way their child can be born inside of wedlock. Ralphs old fashioned that way."

I announced. Nicholas laughed slightly.

"He's practically archaic, if he thinks it's okay to have sex outside of his marriage. Your very kind to agree to the annulment, I'm assuming you had to lie in order to get one. Not every woman would do that for an ex. It does seem like we have more in common than I first thought."

He replied.

"Yes, I suppose so. I just felt sorry for him, I honestly never loved him the way I should have. If I'm being honest, that firefighter you mentioned had a part to play in my marriage not working. He was the guy I slipped up with. Ralph chose to forgive me after I betrayed him. Our relationship had been on the rocks but I should never have gone there, I felt I owed him to some degree.

I revealed. Nicholas was eerily quiet so I decided to change the subject.

"So tell me, why were you such a jackass that day we met in hospital?"

I asked. His face dropped momentarily before his glorious smile returned once again.

"A jackass? Well I didn't mean to come across that way, to be honest I thought you were some stuck up rich bitch. I too made the mistake of judging a book by its cover, it was the way you spoke to me that made me realise how wrong I had been. You wouldn't believe how many patients I have to suck up to because they donate. If I'm being honest, my marriage was suffering so I wasn't in a good place back then, I felt drawn to you which unnerved me."

He replied. Lifting one eyebrow I retaliated.

"I thought you were an arrogant know it all, so let's call it even shall we? Let's start again. I too felt drawn to you, it was more than likely why I was so prickly towards you. I'm not normally that outspoken with strangers."

I said. I raised my hand to embrace him in a handshake. He looked a little confused at first but he decided to go along with it.

"My name is Abigail, I come with a lot of baggage. I'm a single mum to a child I adopted at eighteen years of age. My interests include reading and cyber stalking hot doctors from time to time. I tend to expect the worst, even when presented with the best."

I said. A shyness had been evoked in the handsome doctor as he let my words wash over him.

"My name is Nicholas, I too come with baggage. I work more than I should, my interests include travelling. However I do also enjoy cyber stalking the prettiest of my patients."

He replied but quickly began to back track, realising that it sounded as if he stalked all his attractive female patients.

He fumbled to find a better way of phrasing it. I couldn't help but laugh at him. All of my first impressions of him seemed to be way off, I think I was so determined to dislike him that I was creating flaws where there weren't any to find.

The rest of our date went rather well, we ended up being the last two in the restaurant. As I looked around I noticed the staff cleaning up so we decided to make a move. I had learnt a lot about him.

His parents were originally from Cyprus, they still lived out there. Both him and his brother moved here to study before getting married and settling here. He volunteered as a coach on Sundays with the hospital's junior football team.

Young kids who had been patients once before at the hospital signed up for matches, people would come and join in buying things from vendors who would all donate to charities. That was why he had attended my benefit, he was keen on being involved in 'Differences United' so that he could connect his troubled youths to the programme.

We certainly had a lot more in common than I had anticipated. I decided to end the night at the restaurant. Nicholas had informed me that DNA results were taking longer than expected and would get them to me as soon as he had them.

"Thank You for a lovely night, Nicholas."

I said before kissing him gently on the cheek, as I began pulling away he embraced me in a passionate smooch. His kiss left me tingling all over, I felt as if I was a teenager again whilst in his arms. The grin on his face made me giddy.

"Thank You for giving me a chance, Abigail."

Nicholas replied, he placed his strong arm around me and guided me to my parked car. His car was actually a metre away from mine, yet he still felt compelled to walk me right to the car door.

I wrapped my arms around him, giving him a loving squeeze. We made out for about five minutes before I got in the car and began driving home. I still felt giddy as though I were a school girl, arriving home long after curfew.

Chapter Eleven

I arrived home and nearly walked straight past my son, he was smooching a young blonde girl in the living room. I took a step back, looked over in disbelief before realising what was about to happen.

"Zoe, I presume?"

I said loudly. Startled by my voice the girl jumped up before pulling her shirt back over her exposed lacey black bra.

"Hi Mum."

Simon said; grinning at me cheekily, while his girlfriend practically died of shame.

"How did your date go? I thought you would still be out."

He replied; clearly trying to change the subject, as Zoe buttoned herself up trying to look respectful.

Unfortunately for her, making a good first impression had already gone out the window.

"Clearly not as good as yours."

I said winking at Simon. I made sure Zoe left before heading up to my room.

Zoe was as expected, a typical horny teenage girl. She looked just like Cynthia and Heather back from my teen years, stunning yet clearly vapid. My son was a horny teenage boy, so I couldn't expect much more than for him to follow where his hormones took him.

His birthday was this Friday, I helped my kid book the fanciest hotel room. I'm pretty sure miss black lace would have been happy with the backseat of a car personally, however what the boy wants the boy gets.

There were far worse things he could be getting up to at his age, at least he was open and honest with me about his desires. I had to respect him for coming to me first, he could have just snuck around behind my back.

I was feeling far too loved up to care about my sons 'sexcapades', doctor 'Hot Stuff' was most certainly occupying the whole of my mind. I reached my bedroom just in time to see that Nicholas had text me, he sent me a goodnight text message.

Most men wouldn't dream of texting straight after a date, they wouldn't want to seem too eager. I happily replied with my own goodnight message, I snapped a picture of me in my dressing gown saying 'shame you aren't here with me'.

He sent a reply back with him in his dressing gown too, alongside it he wrote 'say the word and I'm there'. Before I could reply back my phone began to ring, our conversation turned a little naughty as we discussed what we might do to each other if we'd been together at that moment.

After the naughtiness subsided, we ended up having a soppy heart to heart. As much as I had wanted to take it slow, it seems that our new budding romance had a mind of its own.

Nicholas finally agreed to let me go to sleep on the condition that I agreed to meet him for breakfast in the morning. It seemed like a 'win win' situation for me, so I accepted the terms I had been given.

The next morning I woke up early and raced out. Nicholas was true to his words; he was there, sitting in

Rosie's Cafe waiting for me to join him. I swanned over to greet him.

"I know it's only been eight hours, but you are a sight for sore eyes Miss Wilson."

He said, planting a welcomed kiss on my lips as I came close to him.

"So what are we ordering?"

I asked, sitting down painfully unaware of the prying eyes looking at us.

"Oh no, it's that firefighter friend of yours."

He said. Nicholas spoke in a low tone as he gestured behind me. It seems that I had walked straight past Thomas without even noticing him. It took me by surprise how little his presence had affected me in that moment.

"Oh, him."

I said. My face fell. Nicholas could clearly tell something was up.

"Did you fall in love with him?"

He asked, curiously. I hesitated before answering.

"I guess you could say I fell in love with a false version of him, yes. The truth is that I don't honestly know what love is at this point of my life."

I replied. Possibly stirred on by this fact Nicholas leant over and gave me a passionate kiss that left me feeling weak at the knees.

"Perhaps I could show you."

He whispered to me.

I blushed a little. As soon as our order had arrived, Nicholas asked if we could have it to go. He'd received a call, asking him to come into work for a priority consultation.

"Sadly I have to go, beautiful. Duty calls."

He replied before kissing me goodbye. I too had to get to the office so we left together.

"Shall I walk you to your car this time?"

I asked him. We grabbed our coffees to go before heading out of the door.

As we both headed off to our cars, hand in hand, I couldn't help but wonder when our next date would be.

"When can we see each other again?"

I asked. Nicholas pulled me in for a dramatically sexy smooch.

"How about tomorrow night? You can come over to my house, I'll cook."

He replied. That sounded like a rather exciting plan of action.

Chapter Twelve

As soon as Nicholas was out of sight, I got in my car ready to drive off, however a knock at my window delayed my departure. Thomas had decided that he wanted to speak to me, I rolled down the window half way. Annoyed by his presence I tried to get rid of him.

"Can I help you? I'm kind of in a hurry."

I replied. Thomas grinned at me as he bent down to meet my eye-line.

"Just wondering why you didn't say hello."

I shrugged in reply.

"To be honest. I didn't notice you there. Too busy with my new man."

I said. I winked as I put on my sunglasses.

"I meant the other day when you pulled up outside of my work."

I had nearly forgotten about that.

"Did you ever stop to think about the people you hurt Thomas? How many people have you slept with behind your wife's back, I know I'm not the only one."

I said with a coy smile, although I'm not certain I was successful hiding the sadness in my eyes. I revved the engine a little before rolling up the window and driving off.

I felt like a completely new woman, throughout my whole relationship with Ralph I hadn't fully gotten over Thomas. At that moment I knew that Thomas was staying in my past just as much as he was in my rear view mirror currently.

I had no idea whether Nicholas and I had a future or not, but it was nice to know that Thomas would no longer be the one holding me back from finding love. I did enough of that by myself without his interference.

I arrived into work a smidgen late, my mother had beaten me into work once again. Dad had retired from the company years ago, he spent his days playing golf and drinking with his friends. However he did do a ton of work from home for us.

My mum, however, wasn't willing to go quietly. Deidre complained, all the time, about wanting to retire except she could never bring herself to leave. Maybe she didn't trust me to run the place solo, not that I blamed her for thinking that way. I didn't often turn up on time, if I turned up at all.

Especially lately. I greeted my mother despite her grumpy expression.

"Nice of you to join me, Abigail."

Deidre said. Her unhappy demeanor was not going to affect my good mood, not today.

"Pray tell mother, what disaster has befallen us today?"

I spoke in a mocking tone of voice just to add some annoyance to my statement.

"Nothing, I just don't see why you have to be late all the time. It sets a bad example to our staff. You are supposed to be their role model."

She said. My mum sure knew just how to kill my buzz

"Mum, go home and stop worrying so much. I might turn up late occasionally but I always stay late to make up for it when I do. You should take Dad off to see Christina, you can drink mai tais on the beach. These are your golden years, go enjoy them."

I said. Perhaps she would have preferred that I hadn't called her old.

"Abigail, I am not that old yet. How was my deviant sister when you saw her? I haven't heard from her in months now."

She asked. I wasn't sure if I should bare all when it came to discussing Hawaii.

I had been avoiding bringing up my trip out there, she never asked about it so I never brought it up. It was old news now, so maybe it wouldn't be so bad telling my mother.

"Umm… Juliette was pregnant, also she is married to a man named Akoni. He is a local there, he's nice. Probably had their kid by now. Also, Aunty C was… umm, you see… she was drinking again. Juliette assured me she had it under control though, perhaps she's sober now."

I replied trying to divert from the truth bomb I had just dropped on her. Mum grimaced at the news.

"Why hasn't Jeremy called me about this? He shouldn't be letting her drink."

She stated. There was no getting around the truth this time, I'd have to tell her all that I knew.

"Jeremy left her, they got divorced. He's married a local girl, your sister didn't take it very well.

Christina led me to believe you were in touch so I thought you knew all of this already, sorry.”

I replied before leaving her with the new information, I had to get on with work. More to the point she had fallen deep into her own thoughts.

It was close to lunchtime before I heard from her, Deidre had her coat and bag in hand as she hovered in my doorway. My mother stood gazing out of my office window before focusing on me.

“I think a break is needed after all. Let's call it a test run. I'm going to take a month off of work, visiting my sister is much overdue. She sounds like she needs a swift kick up her bum, and you do too. It's time to sink or swim, if you do well then the company is yours.”

She said. I wasn't sure if that was even what I wanted, but I did like a challenge.

“About that, can I hire a manager? It's just that, I honestly don't know if I want the company, I might. I've never tried anything else as a career, that's all.”

I replied honestly. My mum chuckled.

"You remind me of myself Abby, I tell you what. Run the company by yourself for the first week, if you can't handle it then hire a manager. You won't know if it's for you until you try it, will you?"

Deidre said. She had a point, I had been begging her to take a leave of absence for years.

I couldn't really complain now that she was finally giving me a chance.

"Thanks Mum, enjoy your month off."

I replied. Just as she left, Simon decided to pop in to see me.

"Hey kiddo. No Zoe?"

I asked, giving him a sly look before getting up to greet him.

"Sorry about last night Mum, we got a little carried away. She was excited when I told her about the surprise on Friday."

Simon said. I ruffled his hair.

"If you're happy, I'm happy. Shall we go get lunch?"

I asked. Simon had other plans for lunch that included a younger, prettier girl than I; sitting back at my desk I buzzed through to my receptionist. Her perky voice chimed through.

"Hey Cindi. Can you do a lunch run for me? Get yourself something too."

I said. She hurried off, I ate at my desk quite often so she knew just what to get me.

There was a canteen downstairs, the higher up you went in the company the less you paid for the meals. I of course got free food anytime I wanted, the courtesy extended to my receptionist anytime she ordered my food.

It was the least I could do considering she worked so hard, well when she wasn't distracted by her work crush. Some guy in accounting was always hovering by her desk. They would flirt endlessly when they thought I wasn't looking.

Chapter Thirteen

After a busy day at work I was looking forward to hearing from Nicholas. Finally just as I was heading out of the office he rang.

"Hey Abby, How was your day?"

He said. I panicked for a moment after he called me Abby, should I start calling him Nick?

"Good, but even better now I'm on the phone to you."

I replied.

"I know we were supposed to take things slow and we saw each other this morning, but I kind of miss you and wanted to see you tonight."

He said. I was most certainly free, trying not to sound too eager I tried playing it cool. Lowering the tone of my voice I spoke quietly.

"I'm sure I could make time for you, what did you have in mind?"

Nailed it.

"Okay, beautiful. I'll pick you up at eight?"

He asked. Clearly his plans we're going to remain a surprise, I text him my address and headed home.

I got back just in time to see my parents leaving, they were on their way to the private jet. I smiled at them.

"Give Christina my best."

I said. I began waving as they left the grand mansion, it felt pretty eerie without anyone in it.

Simon was out with Zoe, I text him to let him know the house was going to be empty from eight until late. Not that I wanted to encourage him to get it on with his girlfriend, I just would rather he be at home than some place unknown doing who knows what.

After I showered and dressed up, I went to apply my makeup. The mirror had been kinder to me in the past, some grey hair could be seen if you looked closely. Which I avoided doing, from a distance I could be confused for the same image I saw ten years ago.

Aside from a few lines and grey hairs, I was nearly the same girl I once was. I looked at my final appearance satisfied that I had done all that I could.

The doorbell rang, racing to answer it I nearly skidded across the freshly waxed hallway. I quickly composed myself before opening the door; it was Nicholas.

He was a sight for sore eyes.

"You look beautiful, I wasn't expecting such a grand place of residence. I had a little trouble getting past your security."

He said. I laughed as I waved to the security guards staring at my guest.

"Sorry about them, they are overprotective. You look handsome, where are we going?"

I asked. He lifted up a bag of shopping.

"I thought I could treat you to dinner this time."

He said. As much as I was loving the idea of cozying up to the doctor in the comfort of my own home, I had dressed up for no apparent reason. I could have just dressed down into some pjs.

I let him into the house.

"I wish you would have warned me, I'd have made sure I greeted you in my dressing gown."

I said. He pulled me in for a kiss.

"And miss how sexy you look dressed up?"

He asked. His kiss still made me feel weak at the knees, we were getting a little bit handsy when the front door opened.

I had completely forgotten about my son, I told him I'd be out.

"Hi Mum, I thought you were heading out. Is this the hot date you met the other night?"

Simon asked. He and Zoe had just interrupted my very sensual moment with Nicholas.

"Ah, yeah he is. Our plans changed, Nicholas is cooking me dinner. This is my son, Simon."

I said. They shook hands.

"You can join us for dinner if you like? I have enough for extra guests."

Nicholas offered.

"Nah, you're alright we'll just amuse ourselves in my room and stay out of your way."

Simon said, sneaking away with his little blonde friend.

We headed to the kitchen so that Nicholas could start cooking, it was fascinating watching him work. The food tasted good, not chef worthy but that fancy food wears thin after a while. I loved every bite.

"So now dinner is over, what's for dessert?"

I asked whilst winking at my date.

"I wouldn't mind seeing you in that dressing gown."

He said, winking back at me.

"I'm sure that can be arranged."

I said before sneaking us into my room. I swiftly locked the door behind us. He began kissing the back of my neck, I felt like a naughty teenager hiding away in my bedroom.

Nicholas unzipped my dress, I could feel his desire pressing into my back. I turned around letting my dress slip to the floor, pulling him in for a passionate kiss before practically ripping off his belt.

Quickly undressing himself we stood there both in our underwear, I could see his erect penis through his boxers. Undoing my bra I revealed my breasts, he grabbed hold of me pressing his large member against my stomach.

Overcome with desire as he began sucking my nipples I pushed him back onto my bed, I had a strong urge to please him. I climbed on top of him kissing his neck, then his chest, all the way down to his waist. I slipped off his boxers revealing his engorged piece of equipment.

His erect penis was twitching with desire but I wasn't willing to let him inside me just yet. Instead I used my tongue to tease him, he groaned in delight as I moved his penis into my mouth.

I kept going until I knew he was about to reach completion, his whole body quivered as I slipped off my knickers then climbed back on top of him. Before I'd had the chance to place him deep inside of me he threw me onto the bed, it was my turn to be pleasured.

He matched me by kissing me all the way down my body, as he plunged his tongue between my thighs. I couldn't help but squeal in delight. Ecstasy was overcoming me, I needed him inside me right now.

He lifted his head back up, kissing me all the way until he was laying on top of me. I couldn't wait any longer. I grabbed his penis and shoved it deep within me. I wanted him to take me savagely but instead he took his time, I ached for him to never leave my body.

There was no rushing his love making. He wanted to take his time with my body, I must have climaxed at least three times before he finally got going. It was as if he wasn't satisfied in finishing until he had made sure I had been properly serviced, maybe he was just trying to make it last as long as possible.

I felt him ejaculate inside of me, although instead of being reminded of the bad memories from Ralph I was filled with a new found joy. I clung to him tightly not wanting to release his soft penis from my control, limp and lifeless he remained inside of me for as long as I wanted.

We ended up sleeping in each other's arms, still naked and covered in each other's sweat. I'm not sure how long we laid there but I didn't want it to end. After a little nap we both decided to take a bath together.

There was a subtle difference to the way he looked at me, against how other men had in the past. It wasn't just lust in his eyes, he really liked me. I could feel his emotional erection as he washed my back.

He held me like no other had before him.

"That was amazing, I can't even describe how much I enjoyed making love to you."

He said, pulling me round to face him.

"Me too."

I replied. Once we were clean we went back to bed, I fell asleep with his arms wrapped around me.

Much to my surprise he was actually still holding me when I woke up, he looked so peaceful laying there. I turned around to face him, I closed my eyes again only to receive a peck on my lips.

As I opened my eyelids I could see he was wide awake now.

"Last night was fun, can we do it again tonight, my place?"

Nicholas asked. I nodded quietly.

"My house isn't as fancy as this room even, but I think you will like it."

He said. I grinned at him.

"If you're there, I'll love it."

I replied. My morning alarm interrupted our conversation, I turned over to switch it off. As I leaned forward I felt his hand run up along the back of my thigh.

As much as I should be getting ready for work, I just had to have him one last time, I pulled him in behind me placing his hand on my breast. He immediately started kissing the back of my neck and it wasn't long before we'd both been satisfied.

Eventually we got ourselves out the door and on our way to work, as much as I loved sex I wasn't sure if I could do that every night. My legs felt like jelly as I wandered off to my car, it was well worth it for the night of my life.

I managed to get to work on time despite the delays, my staff were waiting with a list of problems for me to sort out. I was beginning to feel a bit envious of my parents; they were sitting on a beach in Hawaii while I was stuck sorting out our company's dramas.

Texting Nicholas was a nice distraction throughout the day, as was a visit from my son. Simon had wanted to see how my date went, he seemed to approve of the new male in my life. I had wanted to ask how things with his love life were going, yet the thought of my little boy 'getting it on' with that girl was a little much.

By the end of the day I was about ready to quit, it wasn't that I hadn't run the office before. In fact I had on many occasions, but each time in the past I knew my parents were just a call away. I was truly alone running the company this time and I'd had to put out more than a few fires today.

I was so keen to head home that I nearly forgot about my plans for the evening. It was when I thought about texting Nicholas that it hit me… I *wasn't* just going to my house tonight. That thought lifted my spirits just a tad. I hurried home yet again like a headless chicken, it seems like I had been going non stop for weeks now.

Simon and I were like passing ships yet again as he left the house, he said that he and his mates were meeting at the cinema. I dressed down for this occasion, not only for speed but also because this time I knew I would be indoors for my rendezvous with Nicholas.

I grabbed some ingredients out of my cupboards and fridge. It didn't amount to much, not to mention the fact I could only make a few dishes. I figured that Nicholas would like the gesture; mac bac and cheese was my signature dish. It wasn't the healthiest of meals (especially considering it was for a doctor), however I owed him a cooked meal.

Chapter Fourteen

I arrived outside of the good doctors door, bag in hand. Unusual as it was to see him so dressed down, I most certainly liked what I saw. I held up my offering.

"I hope you're hungry, I have brought some food to cook."

I said. Nicholas let me in, just as I brushed past him I noticed his niece was here too. Feeling a little surprised, I couldn't help but pause.

"You look lovely and we are both hungry."

Nicholas said as he kissed me on the cheek. The little girl grinned from ear to ear before returning to her drawings.

She had to be no more than ten years old.

"Sorry, I was put on babysitting duty at the last minute. My brother is getting out of hospital tonight, Olivia has gone to pick him up."

He said.

"I don't mind, I love kids. I miss Simon when he was that age."

I replied. I started cooking dinner, thankfully there wasn't much to do for the preparation.

The oven did most of the hard work for me; after it was all in the ovenproof dish I could sit back and relax. I grimaced slightly when I noticed Nicholas was checking out my dish.

"Sorry, it's one of the two dishes I know how to cook. Not very healthy though."

I said. Nicholas smiled at me before pulling me in for a little kiss, his niece began giggling at our PDA performance. Laughing off the attention I focused on the third wheel in the room.

"Well, little miss. What's your name?"

I asked. Her cheeky smile brought me such joy.

"My name is Sophie, I'm nine years old in five months."

She said proudly. After that announcement she returned to colouring in her picture. Crouching down beside her I offered to help her colour in.

She happily let me colour in her unicorns horn, so long as it was pink and purple; of course. I left her as soon as I heard my oven timer go off, racing over to the oven I checked on the food before returning to Nicholas's side.

He hadn't taken his eyes off of me all night.

"You're really good with her."

He said. I shyly shrugged off his compliment.

"Parenthood was my favourite job, sadly I have become nearly irrelevant in Simon's life."

I replied. Nicholas placed his hand on my cheek, there was something in the way he looked at me.

We sat down to dinner and ate the hearty food, Sophie was definitely a fan of my food. She ate it all up before heading back to her pictures, she had moved onto a lovely picture of a princess now.

I hadn't realised that I was staring so much, it was when Nicholas touched my hands that I realised it. His eyes were soulful.

"Tell me about Simon."

He said. I had no idea where to start.

"What's there to tell, one minute he's a five year old and the next he's preparing to lose his virginity."

I said. Nicholas laughed softly.

"What was he like as a baby?"

He asked.

"I wouldn't know, his mum died before I had a chance to find anything out about him. Simon doesn't remember much either so it's almost like his life began at age five."

I said. Nicholas shared a sympathetic look with me.

"His mother took her own life, shortly after dropping little Simon to my front door. I was only seventeen at the time, I had just found out that my ex was not only lying to me about his name. I had a relationship with a fraudster, an abusive fraudster. I shared a bond with Simon instantly, we had both been hurt by the same man when we only craved his love. I met him when he was just four years old, not far from his fifth birthday. I was supposed to go to Uni in America, but Simon had captured my heart. I made a choice there and then, I wanted to

be his mum. No one else could understand him the way I did, although nowadays I feel a distance between us. Even though my ex is his father, I have been the only parent that he remembers."

I continued. I wasn't sure why I was baring my soul right there and then. Nicholas squeezed my hand.

"Is that who's responsible for the scar I saw this morning, Simon's father?"

He asked. I realised that this morning when we made love he must have seen it.

"Ah, yes. Yes that was his doing. I've tried to have it removed, but like my bad memories it still lingers."

I said feeling like I might cry. Nicholas stroked my cheek gently.

"We all have scars from our past, not all of them are visible. They only serve to make us stronger."

He said. I kissed his cheek before retrieving our dinner out of the oven.

Chapter Fifteen

I shook off my past, just long enough to compose myself. It was in the nick of time (pardon the pun), just as well considering that Olivia had arrived to pick up Sophie. I got to meet her husband Scott, he weirdly looked nothing like Nicholas.

I'm sure there was a story there, perhaps they had a different mother. We said our goodbyes, little Sophie left me with the unicorn picture. I waved them off while Nicholas wrapped his arms around me.

"He still needs you, he is just becoming a man."

Nicholas said out of the blue. I realised he was replying to an earlier comment I had made.

"I remember that time well, I never stopped caring about my parents. My brother and I share a mother but not a father, he looks like my dad whilst I look like my mum. A wealthy white man came into my mother's workplace, she was a waitress in a local restaurant. She fell for his charm and the colour of his money, he didn't stick around after that one night he spent with her. I have never met him, the man who raised me married my mum knowing she was pregnant with me. Despite not having a blood tie with him I do love him, he raised me by choice."

He continued. Acknowledging the similarity of his situation and mine I sent him a simple nod. While he was speaking I reflected on the two brothers.

Scott was a big guy, not in the sense that he was a heavy set guy it was just that he was tall and wide. Even leaning on his crutches he was taller than Nicholas, his muscles would look non existent next to Scott's.

He was handsome in a completely different way to Nicholas, his jawline was wide and his hair was curly. Nicholas kept himself clean shaven while his brother let his beard grow long. There were far more differences than similarities, their personalities being one of them.

Nicholas could be charming when he wanted to, however he was a fairly serious guy. Scott was full of jokes, he even mocked the situation he was now in. I could relate to that, I too had my fair share of memories where I used humour to deflect how I was really feeling.

The main thing that I noticed was the fact that Olivia and Scott looked good together, as if they belonged. It was when Sophie stood between them that I finally stopped seeing her as a potential threat, she may be beautiful but her heart was heavily invested in her family.

I had been a little wary of her close relationship with Nicholas, but it was clear to me now that I was the only woman he was thinking about. Tonight we were saying our goodbyes to his family.

They were moving to Spain; Scott had been offered a good job over there, he was going to be co owner of his own practice. An air of heaviness had surrounded him as soon as they left.

"I haven't been willing to admit to my parents my marriage has fallen apart, it's who I was speaking with that day in my office. I want to ask you to be my girlfriend because I see a future with you but it means I have to confess that I'm a divorcee to my parents. They are religious and don't believe in divorce. But after tonight I've decided to come clean and tell them the truth."

He revealed. I was utterly speechless.

"I had no idea…"

I said. He kissed me gently.

"I think we have a lot in common, more than we first thought. It must be why we feel so connected, we both can't have kids and are familiar with brokenness within families."

He said with a pained expression. He had been so open and honest with me so I decided to return the favour.

"I was originally born in America, I never knew about the mansion or my grandma who owned it. Cliff was a close friend to my grandparents, well at least we thought he was. The fact is he orchestrated the demise of all four of my grandparents, he also tried to kill me. In failing that, he sent his son after me. I fell hook, line and sinker for 'Simon', but thanks to my aunt we uncovered his real identity. It was soon after his arrest that I discovered he had been married and had a child, the sicko used his middle name which was also his sons name to trick me. I was fifteen when I met him, so easily manipulated. If it wasn't for my injuries

Cliff inflicted on me I probably would have had his child, against my will."

I said. I grew sullen, morose even.

"I should be just grateful that I'm alive... I am grateful to still be here, of course. Except I have always felt robbed, like I missed out on something special. You know? You must know... you too can't ever have a child of your own. You see, as much as I felt glad I hadn't given Matthew what he wanted, I also lost my only chance. I was actually pregnant once... A miracle... it lasted only a day. That positive pregnancy test had given me such joy until I found out it was an ectopic pregnancy, well it was quite literally the end of the world. I thought that the world was finally being kind to me... instead it was just a cruel joke at my expense. I stopped going to church not long after that experience, I felt as if God himself had betrayed me."

I continued. Nicholas hugged me tightly, I lay my head into his shoulder.

"I'm so sorry Abby, I can't imagine how you must feel. My parents raised me catholic, I haven't been

to mass since my divorce but please don't tell my mother. So I do know what it feels like to lose faith."

He said. After that we sat in a comfortable silence.

Nicholas and I ended up falling asleep on the sofa in each other's arms, we didn't even have sex. The thought hadn't entered our minds, we were just enjoying being close to one another.

Morning came, all too soon we had to face another day. Nicholas's phone began ringing, it was his work. The DNA test results came back negative as Cliffs, it was time for him to get the police involved.

I unfortunately couldn't go into Nicholas's work with him, I had a company to run all by myself. However he promised that he'd update me. I trusted him, I knew that he would do anything in his power to help me.

There was something in the way he was around me, it was as if we were meant to be in each other's lives somehow. I'd even go so far as to say that I was falling for him, if I wasn't so terrified to admit that out loud.

I couldn't believe how intimate we had gotten last night; without even undressing, our souls had connected. Saying our goodbye's at his house we drove our own separate ways, I just kept on smiling over how close we were becoming.

I was knee deep in paperwork when the police decided to turn up, I could see them making their way towards my office. I quickly finished off what I was doing just in time.

"Miss Abigail, we have come to apologise. In the hospital you told us that Cliff Harrison was responsible for your kidnapping, the doctor has informed us of an unexpected discovery down at the prison."

They said. I acted surprised by the news as they continued to tell me what I already knew.

"The man in prison isn't Cliff, we ran his DNA through our system. Luckily we had a hit, as a kid he had a record. He was a foster brat, always in and out of trouble. His name was Robson Billings, he was actually a twin. His brother was called Ronnie Billings, their mother died in childbirth and their father didn't want them after that. Ronnie was adopted, splitting the twins apart. Robson had a learning difficulty which meant no one at the time wanted to adopt him, he ended up in the foster care system. Ronnie became Cliff Harrison late in life, Robson went by many aliases. In fact I'm nearly certain they wouldn't have known about each other, yet that address given to us led us straight to Cliff's twin."

There was no need to act surprised by that information, I truly had no idea about any of that.

After mulling over this new information I just had to ask.

"Have you spoken to the twin in prison yet? He could know some valuable information. He was volunteering to pretend to be Cliff after all."

I said. The officers shared a solemn look, clearly they knew something I didn't.

"We went down to the prison just now, unfortunately someone got to him before us. He's dead, he was shived. The guards can't tell us who did it, somehow they knew to stay off camera."

They said. It had to have been Cliff, he must have realised they were onto him.

"I'm telling you right now, Cliff is behind this. He arranged the murder of Miriam, Matthew and now his own twin brother. The man is evil, you have to find him. Did the doctor also tell you he got Matthew to tamper with my frozen eggs?"

I asked. The officers agreed with my every word, they just didn't know how to track him down. Their reassurances weren't convincing.

"Don't worry, Miss, we will catch him. We always do, eventually."

It was the eventually part that I was worried about. I knew as long as Cliff was free that my family wasn't safe.

If he found out that Simon existed, I'm sure he would try something. They left me alone with my thoughts, I watched them leave as I sat there feeling helpless. I had no way of knowing when he would attack next. For now I'd have to sit back and wait anxiously, sooner or later he would be coming for me.

Before I knew it the time had gotten away from me. I looked up to see all of the empty desks all around me. It was late, I checked my phone and Nicholas had rung a few times. I rang his phone, although as I did I heard a phone ringing nearby.

I looked up and as I did I saw Nicholas standing there, he had a large bouquet of tulips which happened to be my favourite. His warm smile was the first comforting thing I had seen all day.

"I rang your landline, Simon told me you would be here, hard at work. He was right of course, he's a good kid."

He said. I leapt up from my desk into the arms of my very handsome lover, before planting a loving kiss on his lips.

"Careful Doctor Romanos, a girl could get used to this."

I said as I placed the flowers in a vase I had lying around, staff were always needing it for their flowers but now they were being used for mine. Once they were proudly displayed I returned to Nicholas's embrace.

"I've come to take you out, you work too hard."

He said. I laughed, knowing full well he was as bad as me when it came to his work. I followed his lead as we headed out of the door.

Dinner was lovely, we went for a romantic stroll afterwards. Nicholas and I talked about so many things, including our desire to be parents.

"Did you ever think of adopting?"

I asked. Nicholas mulled over my question.

"To be honest with you, yes. I applied to adopt, while I was still married. My wife grew angry over the fact that I hadn't consulted her, I was so desperate to have a child. She wanted a biological child, when I couldn't agree to a sperm donor, she cheated on me. We weren't very good at seeing eye to eye. I actually tried to forgive her for that affair, I felt I deserved to be cheated on as I couldn't give her what she needed. But that fireman was a low blow, she was in it for the sex. We were actually getting on well at that point."

He said. I placed my hand on his shoulder.

"I had no idea she had cheated twice, Thomas doesn't want kids. In fact my ectopic pregnancy was just after I left Ralph for Thomas, the first time I left Ralph. Before our surrogacy troubles we had fallen out of not being able to have kids so I felt safe going back to a man who had no need for kids. When Ralph found out It could have been his he held a small funeral, when Thomas found out he chose to reveal the fact he was married. I do understand how you feel about sperm donors, I felt the same way about the surrogate, I didn't like the idea of another woman carrying my child when I couldn't. I wanted to adopt, Ralph really wanted a

kid with our DNA. Simon has none of my DNA yet I love him as my own. Not that I have my own to compare it to.”

I said. Nicholas saw me shivering a little so he took off his coat, placing it around me he looked into my eyes.

“You and I have been through a lot, and both our marriages ended because of the same fireman. But all of that brought us here and I wouldn't want to be anywhere else right now. Let's go to my place, it's not far from here. I'll drive you to your car in the morning.”

He said. After texting Simon, updating him on my whereabouts, I happily agreed to Nicholas's plan.

There was no more talk to be had, as soon as we made it through the door our clothes hit the floor. We were both satisfied long before we slept, it felt good to be in the arms of this man. As I drifted off to sleep I knew, deep down that I wanted to marry him.

Chapter Sixteen

The day had finally come, my son was turning sixteen. I still remember reading him his goodnight bedtime stories, if I close my eyes tightly I can easily picture him reaching for his favourite book.

Time sure flies by, whether you want it to or not. His mind remained set on losing his virginity for his birthday, my gift to him was the grandest hotel suite money could buy. I sadly had to be at work, I was going to make sure I finished early so that we could share some cake before his big night.

Simon had brought such joy into my life, even though he felt a million miles away at times I knew he loved me. I had done my bit as a mum, now I had to sit back and watch him become a man.

Nicholas reassured me that it was all part of the process, he too was a boy once long ago. I would always see the five year old kid that I fell in love with, he set my heart on fire after his father had tried hard to extinguish any flame I had before that.

Nicholas kindly dropped me to my car the next morning, I met Simon for a quick breakfast before heading to the office. My mother had been off the grid for nearly a week, by now I had finally gotten into my own stride at the office.

Things were running smoothly, the staff were happy yet I never had any time to myself. I had decided that I would advertise internally about a managerial position, a second in command sort of thing.

Instead of advertising it outside of the office, I posted it on all of our staff message boards. I held interviews all day long for anyone who thought they could do the job, no specific qualifications were needed. I just wanted someone with passion, drive and office capabilities.

I had planned to run the interviews for a few days, however on that Friday I found the perfect candidate. She reminded me of myself, a much younger version of me yet I saw a glimmer of who I used to be. I set her to work straight away, she had been working on a lower level, similar to where I started.

Every task that I gave her she completed above my expectations, by the end of the day I had hired her. Whether or not my mum would approve was a whole other matter, but I was very happy with my decision.

Her name was Grace, she worked harder than she needed to and had a hunger for the business. Something which I was lacking of late, with her help I was able to make it home early for dinner. I brought home a small cake that I had ordered from the local bakery, it had a picture of young Simon on the front.

He had been waiting for me in the foyer.

"Thanks Mum, I love it."

He said, before following me to the kitchen. I placed sixteen candles on it, as I lit them I started singing happy birthday to him. Embarrassment mixed with happiness took a hold of his face. Simon blew out the candles in one blow which was fairly impressive.

"I want you to be safe tonight, safe sex yes, but also just take care. Text me before you go to sleep and when you wake up."

I said. Simon laughed at me.

"Alright, can I go get ready now?"

He asked. I agreed as he raced off to go get changed.

He looked so grown up in his suit. Simon had picked a single red rose to give to Zoe, after he takes her out to dinner they planned to go back to the hotel. It would be so utterly sweet if it wasn't my own son doing it, I just wanted him to stay young forever.

I watched him leave with the chauffeur, in the pit of my stomach I felt a twinge. The face of the driver was unfamiliar, I knew the majority of my men's faces. I also noticed a small tattoo on his hand, it reminded me of a tattoo that I saw back at the prison when I attempted to visit Cliff.

It could have been those things but it was more because I didn't like how I felt. I began shouting to my men so that they could stop the limo from exiting. I wasn't honestly sure why I felt so compelled to stop the limo, for all I knew he was just a new recruit yet I'm so glad I did.

As my security team pulled up close to the driver's door, it burst open. I saw a glimpse of the drivers face just before the stranger bolted, my men captured him after a small pursuit took place.

I faced my security team feeling beyond upset.

"How did this happen? I thought our security was tight? How did this stranger get in the driver's seat of his limo?"

I asked. I'm not sure who I was shouting at, I just knew I was furious. The real driver had been found unconscious back in the car garage.

"Simon, are you alright?"

I asked. He ran into my arms, holding him tightly I headed back into the house in order to call the police. I sent Nicholas a text to let him know what had happened, mainly to explain why I couldn't talk. If I hadn't shouted for the car to be stopped, what would have happened to Simon?

I also couldn't help but wonder who the strange man was, could it be that Cliff hired someone after all. He must be stepping up his game, the man literally had no family left now.

Considering the fact he had murdered everyone who had ever been related to him, plus those who had become like family to him, he was completely alone or so I had thought.

The police were no help as usual, all they did was arrest the fake driver and take him in for questioning. They did get the location of where the man was supposed to leave the limo, he had never even met the person who hired him.

They managed to send police to patrol the area searching for clues. Coming up empty they decided that there was no more that they could do. Without proof of Cliff's involvement, let alone his whereabouts it became another dead end.

As they left I saw Nicholas's car pull up.

"What are you doing here?"

I asked. I was pleased and surprised to see him.

"You're having a crisis, I wanted to be here for you."

He said. I held him tightly.

"Thank You."

I replied. Simon seemed a little shaken up so I sent him to go rest, his plans with Zoe were sadly cancelled. Less sad for me than they were for him, of course. I also had requested that he stay in the mansion with my security team standing guard, just until the threat was neutralised.

I did offer to invite Zoe over, incase he felt like having company, but he just wanted to stay in his room. I didn't blame him, I was a wreck and had only been a witness to the incident.

I knew Cliff must have been behind it, I just didn't understand how he had gotten a man in. Unfortunately he used to work and live here, he knew this place like the back of his hand.

Nicholas was being very sweet to both of us.

"Come stay with me, both of you. Until this calms down."

Nicholas offered. I looked straight at him with shock. We hadn't even discussed our relationship status yet now we might be staying under the same roof.

"I'm not sure that would be a good idea, we aren't even a couple yet. Well not officially, and what if you get fed up with us?"

I said. Nicholas got down on one knee.

"Abigail Wilson, will you do me the honour of becoming my girlfriend?"

He asked. I laughed at his silly gesture.

"I do want to be your girlfriend, so if the offer is real my answer is yes."

I said in reply. Nicholas stood up and planted a kiss on my lips to seal the deal.

"So, now we're official. Come stay with me, just for a few days. You can bring a few of your men to watch you, I don't mind. I just want you to be safe. Also, I will never get fed up with you. New surroundings might be just what Simon needs."

He said. I hesitated but only for a minute.

"If that's what Simon wants, I'll ask him in the morning."

I replied. I nestled into Nicholas's shoulder, I felt safe in his arms.

"I know it's early days, I don't want to rush this. But I also know that your the one I've been searching for, I'm falling for you fast. I hope you are too, I can see myself having a life with you."

He said, opening up. I pulled my face up to look at his.

"I feel exactly the same way, I was just too scared to say it out loud. I thought you might think I was crazy."

I replied. Nicholas kissed me to prove to me that he in no way thought that I was crazy.

Chapter Seventeen

After a nice night together, we sat down with Simon. He agreed to come stay at Nicholas's house, I made sure that only my trusted guards would keep an eye on us.

We stayed with Nicholas just until my parents had returned from their trip away, it had been three weeks of bliss when I finally got the call from my parents.

As I looked at my laptop screen I could see that my mother had a stowaway, Aunty Christina was on board the private jet. Apparently my parents had decided to get her clean and sober, whether she wanted to or not.

I waved at the hungover figure laying down.

"Hey, Aunty C!"

I said. She merely glanced over her shades briefly before returning to her sleepy, horizontal position.

"I slipped her something to help with her nerves, she hasn't been back in England for quite some time now."

Mum said. She was always looking out for her sister, even when they were at odds she had wanted the best for her.

"Mum there is something we need to discuss, when you get home."

I said. Deidre looked at me with a pained expression.

"You're not quitting, are you?"

She asked. The thought had crossed my mind in the past but not lately.

"Relax Mother, your company is the least of our troubles. I actually hired a great manager to lighten the load. You will like Grace, I'm sure of it."

I replied. I wasn't willing to get into the real issue over the video chat, not with an already nervous Christina within earshot.

After our conversation had ended I had to then say goodbye to our lovely host, Nicholas was gracious about my decision to leave. I think he would have had us there for longer, I was partly glad to be going though.

It felt far too cozy living the dream, I had gotten far too used to fighting against the world. Simon also couldn't wait to get back to his luxurious way of living, Nicholas's house could fit into our mansion at least ten times over.

I let Grace know that I was going to be late into work, she was of course more than happy to cover. I took Simon to our favourite breakfast place.

"I know Nicholas's cooked breakfast can't be beaten, I just fancied a catch up."

I said. Simon laughed at me.

"We have been living under the same roof for three weeks, barely leaving the house. What could we possibly need to catch up on?"

He asked. I shoved his shoulder gently.

"Fed up of me are you?"

I replied. I teased him before continuing.

"It hasn't been just us, and you have had to put up with my new boyfriend as well. I wanted to see what you think about, everything. I think I'm ready to tell him that I love him."

I said. Simon cringed.

"Not the 'L' word! Well, I like him. I think he's good for you. I didn't ever see you ending up with Ralph, this guys different. Just don't expect me to say that I love him, I'm just not there yet."

Simon joked. After laughing off his dramatic ending aimed to mock me I sat there taking in what he was saying.

Truth be told the 'L' word scared me. The last time I said it and truly thought I meant it, well it didn't turn out very well did it. There was so many things to consider, so much of the future was unknown when it came to us. Changing the subject I asked Simon about his love-life instead.

"How about you and Zoe? Have you rescheduled your little date night?"

I asked. Simon shook his head.

"No, I have decided to wait for someone I love. Or at least like a lot, like you did."

He replied. I looked at him with a crooked smile.

"Oh, I know that my Dad wasn't a good man. But you did love each other, even if it wasn't the right way. When I feared for my life it wasn't Zoe who came to mind, I didn't even think to call her. Just goes to show I can't like her enough to be my first."

Simon said. He was right in his own way, I had spared him from the worst details. I never wanted him to see his dad as the monster that he truly was, his own memories thankfully hadn't stayed with him.

My parents were so happy to see us all, especially their grandson. I left them catching up as I heading into the office, I had planned on sneaking out unnoticed. My Mum was determined to stop me on my way out.

"I'm coming with you."

She said. I turned around raising my palm up.

"No, you aren't. Christina needs you, I have the company under control."

I said firmly. Mum conceded defeat.

"I know, about the attempted kidnapping. I also know you haven't been back to the house since then, my men updated me."

She announced. I had hoped to discuss it with her at a later point in the day.

I scrunched up my eyes before turning back around to face her.

"That's what I wanted to talk to you about…"

I started saying. My mother pulled me in for a hug, a little unexpectedly.

"You should have sent word to us, you didn't have to cope all alone. I've upped our security, upgraded all of the alarm systems to the highest level. I've uploaded all of our trusted guys thumbprints, they will need to use that to access any room of the house and vehicles in the garage. This place is going to be just like a fortress, he won't get anyone in again."

She said. I smiled kindly, she meant well at least. I knew that I would be safe here, the problem was that we couldn't all stay locked up here forever, the very fact that Cliff knew about Simon was my main concern.

How much did he know? He was his biological grandfather, was he here to steal him from me? Either way it was unsettling, to the pit of my stomach I knew he wasn't through trying to get to me.

At work I had a lot to catch up on, I worked into the night to make sure every 't' was crossed and every 'i' was dotted. I didn't want my mother finding fault in anything I had done over the last month, nor with my new managers work.

An unknown number began ringing my phone.

"Hello, who is this?"

Silence met my question as I asked who it was, I was about to hang up when a voice I recognised all too well spoke.

"Kitten, it's me. I need to see you, it's important."

Thomas sounded desperate, every bone in my body told me to hang up.

"I don't think it's a good idea."

I said in reply.

"It's life or death. I'm begging you. I'll be at the bar near your work in ten minutes."

He said. I hung up intending not to go.

For some unknown reason I felt compelled to meet with him. I grabbed my coat as I began heading out of my office, my phone started ringing again. Nicholas was attempting to get a hold of me.

I hung up quickly before sending a message that something had come up. I planned to explain in person what had happened. I'm not sure he'd understand it unless I explained properly.

Before I knew it I was there, Thomas was hiding in the corner crouched over a half empty beer bottle. I sat opposite him inside of the booth, he looked like a broken man.

"Why did you call me down here? You know I don't like this place, not since the day I saw you with your wife. It was this very booth that you sat ignoring I even existed, my heart broke into a million pieces that day. Why would you be so cruel as to bring me back to my lowest point? You better be dying."

I complained. Thomas grabbed a hold of my wrist, his eyes were bloodshot red.

"I'm sorry, take me back please. I beg you. Letting you go was the worst mistake I ever made!"

He said. His grip loosened as he began to cry into his warm beer.

"Why?"

I asked. Thomas looked up confused.

"Why now? Why not before? What's changed? I know you would never leave your wife."

I said. I looked down at his hands, I could see that his wedding band had been removed. It lay on the table behind the drink, I could see a glimmer of gold through the liquid.

"She's left you, right?"

I asked. It felt like a knife had just cut through my chest.

"I caught her in bed with another man, I'm leaving her."

He replied angrily. Fury filled my chest, I felt like screaming. I held back a sea full of tears as I stared at him.

"So! Suck it up, you cheated on her first! With countless women I bet! You have no right to summon me any time you feel sad."

I said loudly. I got up to leave but Thomas refused to let me walk away.

"You do, don't you? Anytime things go wrong you give my work a drive by. What's different?"

He asked. I pulled my arm out of his grasp.

"I love someone else…"

I started saying before he pulled me into a forced kiss.

Chapter Eighteen

His unwanted affection was swiftly rejected, I shoved him off of me as soon as his lips touched mine.

"Thomas, get off of me! You only want me because your wife has seen the light of day, tell me honestly would you truly be begging to have me back in your life if this hadn't happened?"

I asked. He looked at me with sorrow in his heart.

"I get that your life sucks right now. We were just an affair, that is all we'll ever be. You never loved me, I realise that now. I just wish I hadn't wasted years of my life on you! You ruined any chance I had with my husband and now I'm finally happy you do this."

I said. I turned around but as I did I saw what looked like Nicholas, I couldn't be sure so I chased after the man leaving the bar.

I could hear Thomas mumbling some drunken nonsense as I ran out of there.

"Nicholas!"

I shouted. The figure turned around to face me, it was him. He simply turned back around disappearing around the corner, the look on his face was gut wrenching.

He looked at me as if I had just stabbed him in the back, I rang his phone all the way home but it was no use. I wasn't sure which part he was mad at but I knew he hated Thomas.

I couldn't bear the silent treatment, he refused to speak to me. I didn't even know what to say, I wasn't sure what part of that night that he was angry at. What was he even doing in that bar?

None of this made any sense; time seemed to drag painfully. I went on with life, if you could call it living. I spent nearly all my time at home or in my office, a month passed without so much as a hateful text from someone who I had fallen in love with.

It felt as though I had just been robbed of my heart, my chest felt empty. I decided to go to his house, I was fully prepared to bust his door down if I had to. That was until I saw him, he was at our favourite restaurant.

He was sitting across from his ex wife, feeling upset I stormed in there.

"You don't have the right to ignore me Nicholas. If you want to dump me and run back to your ex wife at least be a man about it!"

I said to his table. The whole restaurant stopped and turned around to look at what all the commotion was about. Feeling embarrassed over my outburst I ran out of there as quickly as I had entered.

I'm not sure what it was that he was so angry about, in that moment I too felt enraged by his actions. Another man bites the dust, how is it that I always have the worst luck when it comes to men?

I at least now gave him a real reason to be upset with me, considering the scene I had just made. I gave up trying to contact him and decided to admit defeat. I hadn't done anything worth being dumped but if he wouldn't let me speak to him what was the point.

Thomas hadn't tried to contact me again, I heard from my dad that Thomas and his wife were going through marriage counselling. It was time to let him know about my secret relationship from all those years ago. I had kept him in the dark long enough.

I cleared my throat to gain my father's attention.

"Dad, there is something I need to tell you. It's about Thomas…"

I started saying. I sat down across from my father as he looked at me with such innocence.

"What is it Abby?"

He asked. Thomas was a good friend of my dads, they played golf together still now. I had never been brave enough to tell him about the affair, until today.

If only I had just talked to my dad when we first started dating then I would know about his wife, maybe if I hadn't been ashamed of dating an older man I would have.

Either way my life would have turned out differently, but there was no going back now. I sat there with my stomach twisting into knots.

"Well, spit it out Abby."

He said teasing me.

"Thomas and I, we dated on and off for some time. Ever since the day he rescued me from that tree actually. The last time we were together was just before I married Ralph. I'm not sure why, but I needed you to know that."

I said. Tears began falling, I couldn't talk anymore. It felt as though my lungs would give in if I even tried taking a breath, I inhaled with care as I tried to calm myself down.

My father's voice came through the mist of upset surrounding me.

"Do you still love him?"

He asked. I was a little confused why he would want to know.

"Thomas? I thought I did. I've fallen in love with Nicholas but I think he's done with me now. I stupidly agreed to meet Thomas last night and we got into a heated argument. I think he over heard

most of it. He already knew about my past with him but I lied about where I was going, plus he too has a history with Thomas."

I said. My father cocked one eyebrow as he looked at me, showing his amusement.

"Not like that. His wife had an affair with Thomas. Nicholas doesn't swing that way, as far as I know."

I quickly added. My father chuckled at my embarrassment. I too found it slightly amusing but tried hard not to show it. I was trying to have a serious moment.

"Well, that's quite the mess you made. Give Nicholas some time, perhaps he'll come around."

He replied.

"I don't get it. Why aren't you reading me the riot act, or at least showing how horrified you would be over the fact I'd sleep with any married man let alone a friend of yours."

I asked. Dad chuckled softly.

"I already knew... the way you were around him. Anytime his name was mentioned you would sink into yourself. It didn't take much to put two and two together, princess. Besides, I saw you that night, at Simon's birthday party."

He said. I was in shock.

"I know how Thomas is, but you're a grown woman. I could see how you felt about him. My getting involved would have only complicated things."

William said. His change of behaviour towards Ralph was starting to make sense now.

"My advice to you is to fight for him, he will see your side to things if you give him the chance. If he loves you he will come around."

He said finally. This time I knew he meant Nicholas. His honesty surprised me. My dad truly saw all that? Astounding.

"I didn't think you had noticed that, I tried hard to cover it all up. As for Nick, I guess I'll have to wait and see. I caused quite the scene in a restaurant he was eating at."

I said. William laughed at me.

"You're my little girl, I know you better than you think."

He said, looking at me in a way I had never experienced before. It's like he could see into my soul.

"Did I ever tell you about the moment I realised that I loved you? When your mother was pregnant I was just going through the motions. None of it felt real to me. I put on a brave face for her sake but inside I was a wreck. I was too young to be a father. I even considered doing a runner. But when I held you in my arms in that hospital everything changed. You looked up at me with such innocence, you needed me. Your eyes give you away, when you lie, when you're sad, angry… your eyes always reveal the truth."

William said. He chuckled wryly.

"I knew Ralph was the rebound after I realised you and Thomas were a thing, but if my life has taught me anything it's that you have to learn from your own mistakes. You just need someone stable. Nicholas, he's the real deal. Don't let him slip away. The problem is, you're hanging your head in shame for someone else's sin; *you* are not at fault. Nicholas is probably hurt, but I think he will come around."

He said. I tried hard to process what he was saying, I was still in shock that he knew my secret all along. But his words touched me deeply.

I sat there, unable to focus as I took in all my father had to say.

"It's too late, I saw him with his ex wife. He doesn't love me anymore."

I said. My dad burst into loud, obnoxious laughter.

"Abby, love like that doesn't go away. It lasts a lifetime, that woman doesn't stand a chance against you. Look at your mother and me, we went through thick and thin together. We're still standing aren't we? Don't jump to conclusions and don't give up either."

He said. I smiled briefly.

"What about Christina and Jeremy? They didn't make it."

I asked. My dad furrowed his brow.

"True, that isn't to say that they don't still love each other. Some relationships aren't built to last, others go back and forth like a yo-yo. I saw the way you lit up when you spoke about him, anyone that makes you feel that way is worth fighting for."

He replied. I nodded, he was right about that. I knew there was something I had to do first, something that couldn't be avoided anymore.

I hugged my father tightly, wiping my wet cheeks with my sleeve.

"Thanks Dad."

I replied. I left the mansion in my car, I drove right up to his front door. It was time to rip off the bandaid, I was terrified but knew what I had to do.

I could see clearly that Thomas's wife was home, there was no sign of his car either. I knocked on their front door, his wife answered the door. She was beautiful, I mean she always looked stunning from afar.

Close as I was to her now, I saw just how pretty she was. The last time I was this close I ended up throwing up on her shoes, so I hoped she didn't remember that at least.

She stood before me with no makeup, dressed in her gym clothes. The woman had long curly mousy brown hair lit up by golden highlights throughout, she had a petite frame alongside killer abs.

Her perfectly small features would have you believing she was much younger than her age.

"Can I help you?"

She asked. I inhaled sharply.

"My name is Abigail Wilson…"

I started to say before she stopped me.

"I know you… how do I know you?"

She asked. I was hoping she wouldn't figure it out.

"I had an affair with your husband. It was a while ago now. I actually tried to tell you some time ago but I was drunk…"

I continued before she stopped me again.

"You're that girl, from the bar that night. You ruined my shoes."

She said, seeming more upset about her shoes than me dating her husband.

"I didn't know he was married when I slept with him, I broke up with him after. I've kept it a secret, I was ashamed of what I had been a part of. It has been killing me inside, slap me if you must. I deserve it."

I said as I braced myself for impact.

"You run some charity thing, you live in that big mansion, right?"

She asked. I was completely confused by her reaction.

"Ah, yes. That's me."

I said quietly. The woman eyeballed me for what seemed like forever, I was mid-flinch when she spoke.

"Takes some guts to stand on the doorstep of the wife of the husband you were banging."

She said. I flinched again as she raised her hand, she placed it firmly into position for a handshake.

"If I was going to hit you I would have done it by now."

She replied. I placed my hand into hers.

"Nice to meet you Abigail, please come in."

She said. I kind of feared for my life a little, although her ease of inviting me in was hard to ignore. I followed her into the sitting room, her house was full of art work. I looked at the paintings as I passed them, I couldn't help but notice that they were signed by her.

Chapter Nineteen

Once we had stopped moving I brought up the elephant in the room.

"Sorry about your shoes, was trying to sneak a note warning you about Thomas into your bag."

I admitted. Sonia laughed.

"I wondered what that note meant, unfortunately it too got covered in your sick."

Sonia said. I felt more than a little embarrassed.

"You're quite the artist, Sonia."

I said, trying to change the subject. She smiled at me.

"So you know my name and my address. Did Thomas talk about me or did he just sneak you in here to have sex in our marital bed?"

She said laughing loudly.

"Ah, no. I never had sex here! Thomas was hiding his marriage from me. I saw you together in that bar. It was then that I realised he was in a relationship, I kind of cyber stalked you for a bit after. I just wanted proof that he was with you, turns out you had been married for years."

I replied feeling sheepish. A little humiliated by the truth, I tried not to make eye contact.

"I'm sorry, my husband is a fool. You're a nice girl, you didn't deserve that. No woman does."

She said. I was a little lost for words, I couldn't believe that she was apologetic towards me? Why wasn't she more mad?

"You're not the only one he fooled, he has had at least three affairs. I've finally had enough, I decided to have an affair or two of my own. I made sure he found me in bed with one of them. Give him a taste of his own medicine, you should have seen what a wreck he was."

She laughed. The girl seemed happy over being able to exact revenge on her lover. Despite being at least ten years my senior, she looked younger than me. I could only hope I was as fit as her in five years.

"Yeah, he was a bit."

I said without thinking.

"What!? How would you know?"

She asked. Her lovely features had transformed as she screwed up her face.

"He called me out of the blue, begged me to see him for some life or death emergency. I didn't know it was just to try and get me back, although I'm pretty sure he was just trying to do tit for tat. It meant nothing, I told him to get over himself and go back to you."

I said quickly. The more words I used the angrier she became.

After she had finally reached boiling point her top blew.

"That scoundrel!"

She shouted. I half expected her to swing for me as she clenched her fist.

"I can't believe I fell for his bullshit again, what is wrong with me!?"

I soon realised that her anger was not directed at me but at herself.

"Nothing is wrong with you, I should never have agreed to meet him. I lost the man I love because I did."

I said. I could see tears in her eyes as she unclenched her fists looking at me.

"Why did you? You seem like a nice girl. What made you choose to go see him, even after all he put you through? You must feel the same way I do right now, yet you still answered his call."

She asked. Truth be told, I didn't honestly know why until I began talking with Sonia.

"I wanted closure I guess, he sounded like a broken man. It felt nice to not be the one hurting, I was in a good place. I had finally gotten over him, not the pain but I didn't love him anymore. In fact I realised that I never did, it wasn't him that I fell for because he was never real. He was pretending to be the man that I loved, I actually loved a lie."

I answered honestly. Sonia lent against her kitchen bench quietly, I thought maybe I should leave but I couldn't feel my legs.

What felt like an age passed before she spoke again.

"You're right, he is a fraud. He will never stop cheating, he managed to convince me to go to marriage counselling. As if I was the problem, I never even admitted out loud I knew about the affairs. Now he's ruined you and 'what's-a-face's' relationship too."

She said. He had a way of turning things around to never be his fault.

"Nicholas, Doctor Nicholas Romanos. That's his name. His ex wife also had an affair with Thomas, apparently."

I said. I'm not sure why I felt the need to say his name out loud.

I guess I just missed being able to say it out loud.

"You have got to be shitting me!"

She said. Sonia seemed happy to hear that.

"What? Do you know about that affair too?"

I asked. Sonia looked at me as if I was pulling a prank on her.

"We've met, he came to my door one day. He was looking for my husband, that's how I found out about that affair. His wife's name was Lucille, right?"

She asked. I wasn't sure of her name.

"He wouldn't speak about her, except to say that she cheated with Thomas. I've seen her in passing once or twice."

I said. She went off upstairs briefly before returning back to me, she held a photo in her hand.

As she placed the photo into my hand I could see quite clearly two people half naked, one was Thomas and the other was definitely Nicholas's wife.

"Hurts to see right."

She said. I was surprised that indeed it did hurt not to be the only other woman.

"Actually it's more than that, we were together when he started up this affair. It's my fault they met, he was visiting me in hospital."

I answered. No wonder he was so upset seeing me with Thomas, if he'd gone to all this trouble Nicholas was far more hurt than I initially thought.

I just couldn't understand why he had met with his ex after seeing me fight with Thomas.

"Wow, it's a small world. I've been holding onto these in case I decided to dump his ass. I thought if I balanced the scales he'd either leave or we'd be even. The fact he tried to get in bed with you just shows he will never change. At least not for me."

She said. I agreed with her that he probably wouldn't. She hugged me goodbye before I left her house. She even wished me well and gave me one of her paintings.

We both became a whole lot wiser after meeting with each other. I had a lot to think about, mostly of how to make things right with Nicholas. Not for my own selfish gain, I was beginning to believe he may be better off without me.

Either way, I loved him enough to let him be happy with whoever he chose to love. If he's found it in his heart to forgive his ex wife, than I should respect him. He deserves to be happy, with or without me in his life.

I left a small note and left a gift outside of Nicholas's house. I couldn't see his car so I knew he was out. Hoping it would be enough of an apology I left without looking back. I received no reply sadly, not that I had expected anything from it.

Chapter Twenty

My love life was non-existent, however Simon had started dating a new girl from his school. She seemed to be a lot nicer than her predecessor, Zoe. I actually liked her, so that must be saying something.

It was strange to be on the other end of things; rather than trying to date someone that Simon would like, he was now trying to date someone who I would like.

Grace was impressing my mother at work, she had even given her more responsibility. I was beginning to feel a little obsolete in more than one part of my life. I had lost my sense of purpose.

Every man I had ever loved, since Matthew, had been hurt in one way or another by me. My actual job was being done for me, also Simon no longer needed me as a parent. I spent most of my time alone, but I wasn't sure if that was by choice or not.

Christina had been in rehab since she arrived, we were all visiting as much as we could. Two months passed by, I kept myself busy with work and arranging my annual 'No Means No' fundraiser.

A lot of work still had to be done to get 'Differences United' set up in both countries. So, it wasn't like I didn't already have my hands full with my charity work. Although, I was dreading going to my own benefit alone. Especially when Nicholas would more than likely be there with his ex wife.

Who knows, he could even have re married her by now for all I knew. I desperately wanted to be happy for him, yet there was a Nicholas shaped hole in my heart that just couldn't be filled by anyone but him.

I was starting to think that I was simply designed to be alone in life. However, just when I thought the storm cloud above my head was going to be a permanent fixture, it just so happens that Christina was due out of rehab today.

After a lot of convincing, my Aunty agreed to go as my date. I headed down to the clinic so that I could pick her up, she looked better than when I saw her a few weeks ago. Christina attempted to hide her face behind sunglasses.

"Can we hurry up and get out of here please, in case they change their mind."

She said wearily. I laughed at her urgency to be set free, we soon set off back to the mansion.

Simon and his new girlfriend Anya were both cozied up on the sofa, Christina couldn't stand seeing young love so she hurried to her room. My whole family were invited to my fundraiser, in a matter of a few hours we would all be dressed up and ready for our guests.

I made sure that all of our regulars were invited, including Nicholas and his ex wife. I felt that it was appropriate to try and be the bigger person, I even invited Ralph and his new wife Zoella. I had no intention of speaking to him, but at least I was able to add his name to my guest list.

Sonia and Thomas were invited, not that I thought they would come together. Sonia had stayed in touch, we weren't exactly friends but we were firm allies. Last I heard they were meeting with lawyers to terminate their marriage.

I looked in the mirror at my reflection, I had gone with a more subtle dress this year. I was hoping to blend in with the crowd, even though that might be impossible at my own event.

Looking at my beige coloured, bland dress I felt a bit sorry for myself, it had seemed like my best option until I put it on. Now I just felt like a set of drab curtains.

Flicking through the other dresses I noticed a very bold dress, it was vixen red with dazzling diamonds sewn into perfect positions. I had originally bought it while dating Nicholas, intending to wear it on my next birthday party.

In that moment I decided to stop beating myself up over my ex, if he couldn't even be civil after my kind gesture why should I feel bad? I grabbed the dress in haste, this was my party after all wasn't it? Why shouldn't I stand out from the crowd?

Looking in the mirror again, my reflection had definitely improved. The dress fit every contour of my body perfectly, it was as if the dress had been made for me. I applied matching lipstick, black eyeliner then the rest of my makeup.

I wore my hair down in loose, tousled curls; I felt alive for the first time since Nicholas and I went our own separate ways. Without hesitation I headed off to find my date, she was dressed in a jet black ensemble. It suited her mood.

"If you really don't want to attend my soirée, you don't have to."

I said, feeling sorry for her. Christina just gauped at me.

"I'm dressed now! Not that I could stand a chance next to you, looking like that."

She replied. I took a quick glance down at my outfit.

"You look nice too."

I said, trying to cheer her up. She placed her mascara brush down out of her hand, after a moment of scrutiny she decided that she was ready. Tonight was going to be a night to remember, in more ways than one.

Chapter Twenty-One

The fundraiser did not disappoint, upper class society in its entirety had overtaken our banquet hall. We were holding an auction, Sonia's artwork was amongst the items.

Sonia herself had decided to attend the benefit alone, it seems she wasn't speaking with Thomas currently. However, she also wasn't in the mood for sharing the company of a new man yet, she just needed some time to figure out what she actually wanted.

Sonia told me briefly about her plans for the divorce, I kept my mouth tightly shut. I only allowed pleasantries to exit my mouth, I couldn't even begin to think that I was in any position to give her helpful advice.

I was, sort of, the reason she finally broke up with him, it wasn't my intention but it was now my reality. I tried hard to change our conversation towards a lighter topic.

"Thank You again, for the artwork."

I said. I graciously accepted her final piece for the auction before handing it over to a member of my security.

"It's a shame you didn't keep your piece, I still don't understand why you gave it to Nicholas."

She said.

"I was hoping it could be seen as a peace offering, I wrote a heartfelt note saying that I was sorry and I wanted him to be happy. I'd hoped we could remain friends. But instead I was removed as his friend online for my trouble. I got the message loud and clear."

I replied.

"So strange, last we spoke he sounded like a heart broken man, I was sure he loved you. But at least the painting is in the right place now. He donated it for the auction, so at least you can get some money for it."

Sonia said. This was news to me, but I wasn't willing to upset myself over it. After a brief exchange of words we both headed back to the party.

I mingled with my guests, trying hard not to encounter those who I wished to avoid. Sadly certain people I didn't want to interact with, had other plans. Ralph came over to me as soon as he spotted me, Zoella was here with him and most definitely pregnant.

Spinning around at full speed I attempted to disappear.

"Abby, wait!"

He shouted. I turned back around to witness Ralph out of breath, he had clearly just ran across the room in order to speak with me. I kept my steely glare fixed on him as he spoke.

"Thanks for inviting us, I was hoping to speak with you."

He said. I grew uncomfortable in his presence, perhaps it was too soon to have extended an olive branch.

I pressed my feet forward trying to look taller.

"I'm a little busy, can it wait?"

I asked. Ralph grimaced at my request.

"I thought when you invited me… I guess I thought you were ready to let bygones be bygones."

He replied. I sighed gently under my breath.

"Ralph, I will never get that image out of my head. Besides, seeing the fruits of your labour is a little like salt in the wounds. Zoella just reminds me of everything I've been trying to forget. I can be very happy for you but only from a sizable distance."

I said. Ralph looked at me sympathetically.

"I get it, I do. But we are bound to run into each other from time to time. You've moved on with that doctor guy, I thought you would be happier."

He said. I felt as though I may be sick upon hearing him mention Nicholas.

"Please Ralph, we can talk some other time, okay."

I excused myself leaving an extremely forlorn looking Ralph in my wake. I could easily have just said nothing, I seem to have left my filter behind.

I so wanted to leave my own party, yet again I had no choice but to stay. I made a point of avoiding where all the people I didn't want to see were situated. Nicholas was deep in conversation with his ex wife while Thomas was at the bar on his third drink.

I headed back stage to grab a quiet moment to myself, I decided to look through all of the items we had for sale. Sonia has spoken the truth, Nicholas did donate the painting I had given him. Talk about salt in the wounds.

I made my way onto stage, it was now time for me to introduce my auctioneer onto stage. I glanced at the name that had been chosen supposedly at random by my mother, Doctor Nicholas Romanos was clearly written in black and white.

I inhaled deeply before announcing it.

207

"This year, Doctor Nicholas Romanos will be our auctioneer. Can we all give a round of applause for the completely random choice, as always."

I said awkwardly. I Perhaps didn't need the extra bit in the end, I just wanted it to be made clear that I didn't pick him.

He stepped onto stage looking as handsome as ever, he had put on a very smart suit for the occasion. He smiled towards the crowd as I gave him the gavel, I daren't look into his dreamy eyes.

My makeup was not built for tears, it has been tried and tested in the past so I knew well that my face would be streaming black if I let it. I couldn't tell if he was even looking at me considering I was avoiding looking in his direction.

There was a brief moment where our hands touched, it was like electricity running through my body from his hand into mine. My entire body shook as I heard the words 'Thank you, Abby' being quietly spoken.

I couldn't help but feel as if my life was officially over, I would never again lay in his comforting arms. I heard his smooth voice coming from behind me. But I refused to look back at him, I simply exited stage right without hesitation.

"Thanks everyone, can we please give it up for the beautiful Abigail Wilson."

© This work is copyrighted

He said.

His words were like daggers being dug into my heart. I could still see that look on his face in my mind. Back at the bar he had looked as though I had just ripped his beating heart right out of his chest, the image still haunted me.

I wasn't sure how a man I wanted to marry had become a stranger to me. I also didn't know how he could act like we had never shared a bed together. But it was more than that, I'd never felt closer to a person in all my life.

Even still now his touch was like static electricity flowing through my body. After a few minutes of hiding my mother came to find me.

"Abby, why are you hiding here instead of being on stage with Nicholas. I picked him on purpose so you'd have to talk to him. How else are you going to get him back?"

Deidre said. I had been quietly sobbing when she had come over, it wasn't until she finished talking that she had noticed how upset I was.

She got out a tissue and cleaned my face for me.

"What on earth happened between you two?"

She asked me. I honestly couldn't answer that.

"I don't know. All I know is that I've lost him and my heart is in a million pieces."

I said. I could barely make my words out. Never had I ever felt so much for another person. All my other feelings paled in comparison.

My mum encouraged me to sneak away and let her cover for me. I tried my hardest to stay out of sight. Just as I tried to leave the stage Zuzanna stopped me in my tracks, she had arrived a little late, however had wanted to show her support.

She introduced me to her father, Brian Lambert. They weren't staying long, it was a flying visit. She was due to make a speech after Nicholas had finished with the auction.

I successfully pretended to be okay long enough to hold my own in a conversation, before leaving them in the capable hands of my mother. I was heading over to a quiet corner to hide when Ralph came up to me, again.

I was beginning to rapidly regret my decision to invite him, Zoella wasn't by his side this time at least.

"Abigail, I'm sorry. I don't mean to disturb you again..."

He started saying when he realised I had been crying recently.

"What's wrong?"

He asked. I pulled him in for a hug. I squeezed him tightly before realising how silly I was being.

"Sorry."

I said, pulling away. He pulled me back in and told me everything was going to be okay.

"I didn't mean to upset you, I know how hard it is not being able to have a baby."

He said. His words only served to annoy me. Of course he would think this was about him. I pulled away abruptly.

"You have no idea what it's like Ralph, you have a biological baby on the way. It's easy for you, you fell out of love with me the second you heard your child's heartbeat. I finally found a man to love me even without a viable womb yet despite being

completely faithful I lost him for no apparent reason. Yet you clung onto me no matter how much I hurt you like a noose around my throat."

I said a little loud. Some muttering could be heard in the crowd.

"The icing on top of the cake that is my life, you annul our marriage like it meant nothing yet expect me to play nice when you bring Zoella here. The mother of your child who is carrying the baby who came from your affair. I lost my baby which also flushed away the very last chance I had to naturally conceive a baby of my own. You have no right to ever tell me you know how I feel."

I added. I'd caused quite the stir in the crowd. Even Nicholas had his eyes fixed on me.

I had no idea where all this emotion was coming from, perhaps I did have a large amount of deep seeded issues repressed when it came to my defective womb and love life.

Chapter Twenty-Two

Ralph guided me out into the kitchen as he tried his best to calm me down. Once I had staved off a panic attack I sat on a bar stool with my head in my hands.

He collected two glasses and a bottle of whiskey and brought them over to me.

"I'm sorry."

I whispered as I grabbed the half filled glass.

"Don't be, I like seeing this side of you."

He said, smiling at me. I looked at him feeling rather confused.

"From the moment I met you I saw this unattainable goddess. Do you know how many women wanted me, simply because I had money and a fancy restaurant? You on the other hand rejected me, even cheated on me."

He said. If he was trying to make me feel better he was doing a terrible job.

"Thanks Ralph."

I said sarcastically, before taking a large sip of my medicine.

"You don't get it Abby, you weren't in love with me and that was what attracted me to you. Too many woman threw themselves at me for all the wrong reasons. Not being able to win you over kept drawing me to you. When we got married I felt I had you and my desire to be a parent overtook my desire to keep you. Zoella and I connected on an emotional level, I'd confused my feelings for you as something more than they were. Our relationship wasn't right for either of us, I am sorry I ended it so abruptly."

He continued. I screwed up my face in response.

"What I'm trying to say is that it wasn't your fault. I would never have known how important having a kid was to me without going through that with you. I agree it was wrong to ask for an annulment, even I was sad that our marriage went away like it never happened."

He said. I was starting to get where he was coming from.

"I didn't fall out of love with you Abby, still now I definitely care about you but we weren't meant to be. You and that doctor have that special something we lacked. I can't honestly say I have that with Zoella but I know I'll never leave her."

Ralph said finally. I finished my drink, praying he would stop speaking. When he finally did I wasn't sure what to say.

I looked at him, directly in the eye.

"Nicholas doesn't love me, he hasn't spoken to me in months."

I said plainly. Ralph laughed a little.

"I have no idea why he isn't speaking to you but trust me, that guy is crazy in love with you. I see it in his eyes."

Ralph replied. He finished his drink and left me to wallow in my own self pity.

I closed my eyes tightly taking in five deep breaths, this was agony. I heard a loud clattering noise coming from the pantry cupboard so I decided to go investigate. Simon and Anya were hiding in their half naked, clearly I had interrupted them when I came in here with Ralph.

"Hi, Mum. We were just getting a snack."

Simon said, clearly lying. It was obvious they had been hiding so I wouldn't discover them.

"Yeah, I'm sure. Well why don't you and Anya get dressed."

I said, trying not to smirk. They grabbed their clothes and started heading out of the kitchen.

"Simon, next time keep it in your bedroom."

I added. Simon looked so embarrassed.

"Where's the fun in that?"

He said with a cheeky smile. I shook my head in disbelief as the nearly naked pair left the room.

It was nice in a way to see his carefree nature in full force, I had never had such a free experience when I was young. My smile soon faded when I turned around to see Sonia standing before me looking terrified.

Her husband was looming over her shoulder. Sonia tried to mouth the word 'run', unfortunately before I realised what was happening it was much too late.

Thomas was steaming drunk holding a weapon, it looked like a small pistol was being pointed at Sonia's head. Thomas spoke with a hateful tone of voice emanating from his venomous mouth.

"Thanks for the invite, bitch."

He said. I couldn't believe the state he was in.

"Thomas, what are you doing? Put the gun down!"

I screamed. He shoved Sonia forward so that she was standing next to me, he quickly had the gun raised in front of my face. I held Sonia's hand trying to comfort her.

"You told my wife lies, tell her the truth. I didn't touch you! You're the reason she won't take me back."

He said slurring half his words. I had to talk him down somehow.

"If I tell her that, will you put down the gun?"

I asked. Thomas grabbed a hold of me in anger, while he was focused on me I urged Sonia to run so she could go get help.

She ran out of the door behind me, he raised the gun up to shoot at her but missed her entirely. Unfortunately for me, he didn't miss everyone. His drunken aim had caused the bullet to go straight into my shoulder, I shouted in pain as he looked at me confused.

The alcohol had made him completely delirious, I fell down leaning against the counter.

He continued on as if he hadn't just made me bleed.

"Why did you do it Abby? Taking my heart wasn't enough, you had to take my wife away too."

He said before throwing something at me, I grabbed it with my left hand, wincing in pain as I looked at it. It was my note, the note I left for Nicholas. The one I had left outside his house on the painting. It was hard to speak.

"How the hell… do you have… this?"

I struggled to ask. Thomas crouched down beside me.

"I saw you in my house so I followed you, if I can't have you then why should he get to have you? I replaced your note with one of my own."

He said laughing at me. I looked down at the words I had written, the note read as follows:

Dear Nicholas,

As much as it breaks my heart to see you leave, I want you to be happy even if it isn't with me. Before you make your decision you should know all the facts. I'm sorry for hurting you. If there's anything I can do to make up for it I will. I'd move the world if it meant having you back in my arms. You see I've fallen in love with you, if you don't feel the same way about me I'll understand.

Hope to hear from you

Abigail Wilson.

I looked back up at Thomas. I Honestly didn't know what was hurting more, my shoulder or my heart.

"Wanna know what my message said?"

Thomas asked. I was terrified of what Thomas might have said to him. He sat down beside me as he showed me a photo of the message Nicholas had read thinking it was from me. His message said this:

To Nick,

Sorry to do this but I don't want to see or hear from you ever again. I don't love you. I hope you understand, you should move on with your life and forget about me.

I couldn't believe it but I was too weak to complain. I began to feel hazy, in a blur I saw my security men come rushing in, shortly followed by Nicholas.

Thomas had already given up before they came to get him, the gun was in a pool of my blood. I was losing a lot of it. I kept blacking out but I was able to stay lucid long enough to hear Nicholas speak.

"You're gonna be just fine Abigail, I've got you now."

Thomas got hauled out by my men, my dad looked at him with disappointment as they carted him away.

The last thing I remember was being held in Nicholas's strong and capable arms, but as my strength faded so did I. Keeping my eyes open had become just a little too challenging for me, I felt safe there in the arms of the man that I loved.

Even if this is the last time he would ever hold me. Flashes of Cliff, Matthew and all the horrid memories that came along with them surrounded me while I was unconscious. They were all around me laughing at me, incessant laughter while I span around trying to block out their noise.

All went quiet, I peered up and saw the face of Grandma Jean. She was smiling down at me whilst extending her hand, she didn't need a cane to walk anymore. She shone brightly like an angel.

"Come on Abigail, you are stronger than this. Fight."

She said, using her hand to pull myself up I nodded in agreement. I was strong, I had survived worse than this. With or without Nicholas, I had to keep fighting for a better life. It wasn't over yet.

I woke up yet again in hospital, what was it with me and hospitals? They clearly liked me, even though the feeling was not mutual. My dad was sitting in the chair next to my bed, I felt a little groggy and my shoulder still hurt.

"Dad?"

I said. He looked up from the newspaper he was reading, placing it down he stood up beside me.

"I'm so sorry Abby, I had no idea Thomas would ever do such an awful thing. How are you feeling?"

He asked. My right arm was tied up in a sling, I tried to touch his arm with my left hand but it too seemed a little out of sorts.

"It's not your fault, no one could have predicted that he would get drunk before crashing my party with a gun. I just don't understand how he got one passed security."

I said. Dad had a sheepish look about him.

"It's *my* gun Abby, I got it a while back... for protection. I never intended on using it, I just felt safer knowing it was there. Thomas was the one who helped me acquire it, that's how he knew where it was."

He said. It made a little more sense now, perhaps he came to my party to confront me but needed some liquid courage.

"Nicholas did a great job patching you up, we're lucky he was there. You should have seen him in action. He stopped the bleeding and carried you out of there before driving you to the hospital himself."

He said. I smiled in reply. I still couldn't get over how Thomas had behaved. Alcohol had a nasty habit of bringing out the worst in people, that was also true of Christina. Although he was likely sober when he switched out my note for his.

Thankfully my Aunty had stayed sober for the entire night, fairly impressive considering she had full access to an open bar. Although we already told all of our bartenders not to serve her any alcohol, in case she tried it.

My dad continued catching me up on the night's events after I was whisked out of there, all the items up for auction were sold. We raised half a million in total for the 'No Means No' foundation, double last year's donations.

It perhaps was due to the fact they heavily sympathised with their host.

"Perhaps you should get shot every year."

Said William, trying to cheer me up.

Nicholas came to see me so my dad made an excuse to leave. He wasn't here as my doctor in this case in fact he came to see me without his white coat on. He had my note in his hand. I guess he finally read it.

"We have to stop meeting like this."

I said, trying to lighten the mood. He smiled as he sat beside me.

"I know Thomas changed the note."

He said. Try as I might I had no worthy reply to give him.

"I'm sorry, Abby."

Nicholas simpered. Why was he apologising to me?

"If anyone should be sorry, it should be me, Nicholas. I know it's too late for us."

I replied. He held my left hand tenderly.

"I have a confession to make, about that night you met Thomas. I followed you to the bar. I let my jealous nature take over because of my history with my ex wife. I let my past cloud my judgement."

He said. I wasn't sure where he was heading with this but the fact his ex wife was still his ex gave me a little hope.

"I saw some of your conversation, I realised in that moment that I was in love with you. I felt so ashamed that I had followed you there. You did nothing wrong."

He continued.

"I don't understand, you looked at me with such hurt in your eyes that night."

I said feeling confused.

"I didn't feel I was good enough for you and sunk into depression, not for the first time. I went to see my ex wife to try and get some closure. After you got mad at me I had every intention of trying to make it right with you until I read that note."

He replied.

"I should have known it wasn't you that wrote it, I just assumed after you saw us in the restaurant you were upset with me, enough to end things. If I'd realised sooner, you wouldn't be in here right now."

He said finally. He seemed to be blaming himself for everything that happened.

I squeezed his hand gently.

"I still love you, none of this is your fault. I know all too well how crippling depression can be."

I replied. He looked as though he might cry.

"Are you back with your wife?"

I asked. Nicholas began laughing.

"Abby, I'll let you in on a secret. I wasn't trying to set you up with Burt. That day in the hospital I was flirting with you, terrible as it was due to the fact my marriage wasn't over yet. In fact she hadn't cheated on me yet. But deep down I knew my marriage was over. I tried to convince myself I didn't like you. Since that day my feelings for you have grown and now it's safe to say I'm completely in love with you."

Nicholas revealed. I tried to contain my happiness over the news.

"So, what does this mean... For us?"

I asked, feeling hopeful.

"Well if you love me and I love you I think that makes us a couple of people in love. I want you to be my girlfriend again, if you want to."

He said. I had a cheeky smile on my face.

"I'd like that, but only if you promise not to shut me out when you feel depressed again? I don't just

want the good parts of you. We all have our good and bad sides, I want you to be able to share everything with me."

I said. He planted a kiss on my lips. I kissed him back with all the passion we had shared before.

I completely forgot we were even in the hospital until the nurse barged in, shortly followed by the rest of my family. Nicholas decided to leave me to it, but he promised to come see me later, he was working tonight on purpose so that he could take care of me.

My mum, in particular, was very pleased with the fact that we were back together again.

"So, I see that you and Doctor Gorgeous are back together."

She said. I poked my tongue out at my mum, she loved interfering in my love life any chance that she got.

Chapter Twenty-Three

My family left so I could rest, it wasn't long before I was all alone in that hospital bed again. They had fussed over me for as long as they were allowed, especially Simon who just wanted to make sure that I was comfortable. He fluffed my pillows and made sure everything was within my reach.

The nurse asked them to leave once visiting hours were over, after more affection they agreed to leave me so that I could rest. I must have dozed off for a few hours after they left, when I woke up it was pitch black outside.

I switched my light on so that I could get my bearings, the hospital was a ghost town. I saw a shadowy figure in the window, I felt a cold sweat come over me. Not knowing what to do I jumped out of bed, running around the corner I could see Cliff.

He kept laughing maniacally holding a gun, every time I tried to chase him down the hallway would stretch longer. I felt a hand on my shoulder that made me jump out of my skin, I looked around again and Nicholas was standing above my bed looking worried.

I seemed to have been having a nightmare.

"Are you alright? You were groaning in your sleep, you became quite restless too. You look pale."

He said. Well I did just get shot, perhaps this was a side effect.

"I was having a bad dream, it felt so real. Cliff was here, I tried to chase him but I couldn't catch him."

I replied. Nicholas's silence proved he was especially worried about me, he was back in his white doctor's coat now.

"I think you could use a break. How about I take you and Simon on holiday? I have been meaning to visit my parents anyway."

He offered. I was about to protest, after all I had gone through recently I didn't have the energy to fight his kindness. Instead I wholeheartedly agreed, I did need to get away from the stress I had been put under.

So much had transpired in the last six months, what could possibly go wrong? I told Nicholas to surprise me with all the details, I couldn't wait to see what he had planned.

A surprise it certainly was, as I arrived at the airport not knowing my own holiday destination. I couldn't help but feel a little nervous. I had just endured a long winded goodbye between Anya and Simon, you would have thought he was being shipped off to the army the way she acted, it was a two week holiday!

Young love, certainly nothing like what my first love had been like. Feeling bad over being the reason for their forced time apart, I did the most irrational thing. I immediately suggested that she join us on our holiday, what is wrong with me?

So now it was going to be a couples trip of sorts. Nicholas was incredibly understanding over the whole debacle. I would have preferred to use our private plane, however Nicholas insisted on us using the public flying services available.

First class was nice, it pales in comparison to our plane but it would have to do. Anya acted as if she had never been on a plane before, she kept 'goo gaaing' over the large spacious chairs. The in flight announcements revealed our destination finally, I had been kept in the dark for weeks now.

We were traveling to Cyprus, Nicholas was originally born there but moved to England when he was just a teenager, he and his brother stayed with relatives so that they could educate themselves here.

I had never traveled to Cyprus before, it was a beautiful island filled with holiday resorts and beaches. We drove past many places I would die to stay in only to wind up deep within Cyprus instead, he insisted that we stay nearby to his family.

I would have even been happy staying in one of the small orange roofed houses lining the hillside, we did not stop until we reached an extremely poor secluded area. The houses there were similar to the nicer ones we had passed, there were only a few rundown huts surrounding the one we were expected to visit.

I didn't quite understand why a wealthy doctor would allow his parents to live in such a poor quality of living.

"Mum, Dad. This is Abigail, Simon and Anya.."

He announced. His parents practically leapt for joy at the sight of their new guests. They began kissing and hugging us all. I had expected a little more hostility considering what he told me about his mum's feelings on divorce.

Once I had been allowed my own personal space again, they began gently arguing about money. It seems that his parents were living here against Nicholas's wishes. In fact he had apparently sent money many times before yet they refused to take it.

They sent him along with his brother to England to live with his Aunty so that they could have a good education and better quality of life. As soon as he had the chance he began trying to provide for them, they were proud and wanted no hand outs.

The area they loved had been abandoned years ago, it was to be a developmental site for new housing. The houses that remained were the only ones who had refused to sell their land, so they built around that small area despite their protests.

"I was born in this house and I will die in this house"

Said his Mum. A touching sentiment had it not been for the crumbling bricks and broken roof. I admired them for their determination, they had been faced with much hardship yet stood strongly by their beliefs.

I was just beginning to get my head around the idea of potentially having to stay there in their cramped living quarters when I heard the good news, Nicholas had in fact rented a nearby house for us to stay in instead.

I tried very hard not to let the relief show on my face, I didn't want to seem ungrateful or spoiled over our fully paid trip away together. The house we were going to stay in was much nicer, not as nice as the grand hotels by the beachside but it was clean and cosy all the same.

After seeing where we could have been staying I was just grateful for the clean running water, not to mention an actual kitchen, bathroom, bedrooms and living room.

We visited all over Cyprus, Nicholas took us to every tourist destination going plus all of his favourite places from his childhood. It was so nice to spend time in his world, I was relaxed and enjoying my time away from my stressful life back home.

As much as I loved my life, it had been filled with a lot of drama not to mention stress lately. Simon had a great time, I barely saw him as he was always off with Anya somewhere. It gave Nicholas and I plenty of time alone together, by the end of the trip we were just as close as we were before the fight if not closer.

"Nicholas, thank you for the lovely trip. It was just what I needed."

I said. We sat there on the small balcony watching the sunset.

"I had something I wanted to ask you…"

Nicholas said as he reached into his pocket, he knelt down on one knee. Looking up into my eyes with a nervous smile he continued.

"… Abigail Wilson, I love you…"

He revealed an opened ring box, inside was a very unique diamond ring, it was surrounded by smaller diamonds in the shape of a circle.

If I had to guess I would say it was very expensive, the white gold set it off perfectly. It certainly beat his joke proposal over us becoming exclusive.

"Yes!"

I shouted prematurely. Nicholas laughed at me.

"You didn't give me the chance to ask you anything yet!"

He said. I tried hard to contain the excitement brewing up inside of me, I felt as if I may explode.

"Abigail Wilson, I love you very much. I want you to be my wife, will you marry me?"

He asked. I couldn't even get the word out again as I nodded, tears were trying hard to escape as I placed my hand out for him to put the ring on my finger, it fit perfectly.

He stood up as I looked at the immensely attractive ring now firmly on my finger, I wrapped my hands around his neck pulling him in for a passionate kiss.

I would have wanted to make love to him there and then if it hadn't been for the interruption, Simon and Anya had just arrived back at the house. Simon's mocking voice could be heard through our smooching.

"Alright, you two. Get a room already."

Simon said. He snickered at his own joke, I placed my hand in his face. Intentionally I showed off my new bling.

"Nicholas proposed and I said yes."

I announced. He paused for a minute, I wasn't sure if he was happy or not. He began joking again.

"Just don't expect me to call you 'Dad', alright."

He replied. They both smiled awkwardly before shaking hands.

"You better take good care of my Mum."

Simon said. Nicholas nodded accepting his request.

I couldn't help but feel he was holding back just a bit, I wanted to pull him aside but he quickly excused himself and Anya as they both headed to their bedroom. I didn't let it dampen our mood, we quietly snuck off to our bedroom so that we could make love.

Chapter Twenty-Four

The walls were pretty thin so we had to be quiet, not an easy task with Nicholas considering how good the sex could be. After a few hours we managed to drift off to sleep, tomorrow was our last day here so we were packing up and saying our goodbyes.

I knew he must have bought that ring before our trip, I wasn't sure as to when he could have decided that he wanted to marry me. After we had packed up the car, I caught myself staring at him.

"When did you buy the ring? It looks custom made."

I asked. Nicholas grew a little shy. He looked at me in a way that made me feel guilty, as if I had just been caught with my hands in the cookie jar.

"Before we broke up, the day you left to go back home I had it ordered. I was going to propose, I've kept it on me ever since. I guess I never gave up hope. It was when we were sitting together watching the sun go down, I saw a glimpse into our future. At that moment I felt that it was finally the right time, for both of us."

He replied. I finally understood, all of it. He saw me as his future wife, the time we spent together in his house had led him to see a future with me.

While he had been making plans for our life together, I was left worrying that we were getting too close too quick. To be fair I had been burned often in relationships, you can't blame me for always waiting for the other shoe to drop.

I looked deep into his eyes.

"I'm so sorry. You're right, I wasn't ready before. It's possible that agreeing to meet with Thomas was my way of subconsciously self sabotaging our relationship. I'm not sure but I do know that I am

ready now, I just wish that we hadn't lost all of that time."

I said. Nicholas smiled widely.

"We have the rest of our lives together, in sixty years we won't even remember that small time apart."

He replied. I couldn't help but smile at the idea of us in sixty year's time.

"Just promise me we won't be as stubborn as your parents, I'm happy to move to a new house."

I said. He laughed.

"Actually I was hoping you would say that, I want us to buy a house together. I can't see myself living in that grand mansion, as nice as it is. It doesn't feel like home, I want us to build a home together. Maybe adopt a kid or two in need of a good home."

He said. I was taken aback by his suggestion.

"That would be really nice, I have never truly wanted to adopt another child but for you I would. You would make an amazing Father. I was mostly afraid of doing it alone but since meeting you I no longer have the fear that I'd be alone to raise a child."

I said. We embraced before summoning the young love birds to the car, it was now time to say goodbye to my future in laws.

My stomach was in knots the whole drive there, what was in reality a twenty minute drive felt timeless. I waited patiently while Nicholas told them the news, his mother hugged me so tight. I felt as though I would never breathe again, when I finally got free his dad decided to attack me with love.

I hadn't ever experienced anything so full on before. Most of my boyfriends parents were out of the picture or just didn't care much who their son married. Tears were shed, promises were made, soon we were driving to the airport for our flight.

I felt as though I had just been welcomed into his family, not superficially but honestly and truly I was now seen as their relative. The memories of this holiday would be etched into my mind forever.

All in all the getaway adventure had been exactly what we all needed, I tried to get Simon alone at some point during the trip unsuccessfully. Anya and Simon had been connected at the hip for the whole holiday, not that I could talk considering my blossoming relationship that had been taking up most of my spare time.

I sat down thinking hard about what I could say to him.

"Are you alright? You seem preoccupied."

Nicholas asked. I looked up at him, I had apparently been staring at the happy couple.

"Lately I have been feeling a distance between us, Simon has this new girl in his life. I feel a little... I don't know. Unneeded perhaps?"

I revealed. Nicholas laughed at my concern.

"He is becoming a man, he will always need you. It's part of growing up, maybe we could start a family of our own after we're married. Give you another young and impressionable child who needs a mum just like you."

He said. I liked the sound of that. I rested my head gently on his strong shoulder. I felt like one life was ending yet at the same time a new one awaited me on the horizon, it was a crazy feeling of sadness and happiness all rolled into one big bundle of confusion.

I had never truly considered what it would feel like to find 'the one', I had spent my whole life looking for this amazing guy who I can share my life with. Now I was here, the world was at our feet. My new normalcy had overtaken me in a strange way.

I had nearly given up on ever finding someone to love for real, I had held out hope. All the same I still doubted it was the real deal when it came along. Life had a funny way of surprising me, even when I thought I had seen it all.

I had read every romance novel going, I never thought about the aftermath of actually finding the guy. With Ralph I just went through the motions, not truly caring what happened next. I now found myself faced with many options, I could truly have everything I had ever wanted.

Including things I never even knew were my deepest desires, Nicholas had given me everything that I never even knew I had wanted so badly. Adoption hadn't been a priority before, I was just happy with raising Simon.

Yet now it had become something that struck great happiness just thinking about, to raise a child with the man that I love; priceless.

"I seem to be warming up to that idea more and more."

I said, speaking softly. As Nicholas held me I felt cozy in his arms.

"I can't wait to see what tomorrow brings."

I added. Nicholas wholeheartedly agreed.

Chapter Twenty-Five

Reality had clunked me right on top of my head. I was getting married, the wedding was a week away. Months had passed me by as if it had been no time at all. I was going to say I do and become Mrs Abigail Romanos.

Running a company, planning a wedding and looking into adoption was a full time job. I had quite literally no time to even breathe, let alone enjoy myself.

I had all but forgotten about Cliff lurking around every dark corner, there was too much to think about. I set the wedding up in an extremely secure location, we would be guarded by more security men then I could count.

There was no way *that* man was going to attempt the same thing twice, I wasn't going to risk him ruining *this* wedding. Nicholas was about as helpful as a fried egg when it came to wedding decisions, he just wanted me to be happy.

I just wanted the day to be over and done with, the stress was just too much. Not to mention the fact that my dear father had decided to take it upon himself to invite my cousin, to be fair she was his niece however I was still not a fan of hers.

I hadn't seen her since I was a teenager and any stories I heard about her from my dad didn't help me like her any more than I did then. I just didn't get on with her, as a person she was shallow and vindictive with a side of upper class snobbery to boot.

They were due to arrive at the manor any minute, her parents were bearable at least. Heather Miller was unsurprisingly still single, she had set her sights very high when it came to marriage.

A little too high in my opinion, she wanted to marry a rich and famous somebody so that she could spend her days shopping and gossiping instead of manual labour of any kind.

So far she had only managed to become the girlfriend to a singer who was said to be the next big thing, only to wind up being a one hit wonder. Here I was yet again awaiting the arrival of the girl I once loathed.

I was tempted to contact Patricia for old times sake, however looking at her perfect family portrait put me off. We used to have such a great time mocking Heather, never to her face seeing as she terrified us. Still to this day her name sent shudders down my spine, as did her steely gaze.

Her arrival did not disappoint, she swanned in pulling the smallest suitcase in the world along behind her. I was about to compliment her on the fact that she brought such little luggage with her, luckily my staff stopped me as I saw them lugging her ridiculous amount of carry on luggage shortly behind her.

She looked exactly the same as the last time I saw her except for longer hair, six inch heels and flawless skin. Her shrill voice bounced against my eardrums as she announced her presence.

"Abigail darling, have you been stress eating again? You have got to join a gym, it's not healthy you know."

She said before kissing me on each cheek in a dramatic fashion. I gritted my teeth, it was all I could do to contain myself.

"No Heather, I am not 'stress' eating. I weigh the same as I did ten years ago. Not all of us can have your figure, now can we? Did you plan on staying long?"

I replied with a force smile applied firmly to my face. Her snide laughter was enough to send you doolally.

"Not without hard work and commitment, I work hard for my figure. If you want me to teach you my routine just let me know. Toodles."

She retorted.

After our brief encounter she headed off to one of our many guest rooms, leaving me to show her parents around the manor. I had no idea why I let her get to me, it wasn't like we were kids anymore yet she still knew just what to say to wind me up.

I was not looking forward to dinner, my dad had insisted on having a family sit down meal. Simon had invited Anya for moral support, I of course had Nicholas for mine.

Despite her regular calls to my father she felt the need to catch us all up on the new aspects of her life. Heather had now become a reporter, she interviewed stars at red carpet events.

I could only assume she got into the field in order to gain a husband, unsurprisingly she was now engaged to her boss. Apparently it was love at first sight which happened less than a month ago.

He was a wealthy recently divorced owner of the famous magazine that she now worked for. 'Glam Central' was the title of the one she wrote a column in. Although knowing Heather like I did it wouldn't surprise me if she'd split up his marriage to get him.

Her boss wasn't who I had imagined her with, I researched him on the web as soon as she mentioned his name (discreetly of course). He was a silver fox, he looked like the 'all business' type from his pictures.

Perhaps that's why his first three marriages hadn't panned out, not that it should bother her considering she worked with him. She seemed happy with her decision at least, her parents gleamed with pride at her every word.

After the meal was over Heather made a b-line for me, Nicholas was on call so had to go back into work as there was an emergency. An essence of dread could not be shaken as I stood there watching her purposeful strides, she was annoyingly graceful as she sauntered across the room.

She was the picture of a glossy magazine cover, even in her business pant suit she oozed charisma. It was as if she had walked to me in slow motion, I didn't know what to expect. I couldn't judge her face, it was always pulled into a perfect smile.

Not a joyful one but her shining white teeth could be seen nonetheless.

"Caught yourself a dreamy doctor I see, what happened to the lame chef?"

She asked. As much as I wanted to come back with a witty reply, I had nothing but the truth to offer.

"Irreconcilable differences, he wanted kids and I couldn't give him any. Our surrogate couldn't wait

to give him a biological child of their own. Apparently doggy position worked wonders for them."

Heather shrivelled up her small nose in disapproval.

"If everyone gave up on relationships that easy, your parents would have divorced long ago."

She announced. Her words hung in the air, I wasn't willing to accept them. What the heck was that supposed to even mean? My parents have never cheated on each other... had they?

I certainly didn't have any siblings I was unaware of... did I? I stared blankly at Heather disbelieving her ridiculous words. Besides, after my heart to heart with William I'm sure he would have come clean about any issues like that, right?

"Oh, come on. You must know all about that woman, Ronnie? Your dad nearly divorced your mum before he decided to stick with it."

She continued. Enraged by her deceit I denied that it could ever be possible.

"You're lying, my dad would never cheat on my mum!"

I replied angrily. I was fairy insistent for someone who doubted her own words, what if it was true?

"Sorry, Abigail. I honestly thought you knew, Toodles."

She said without a care in the world. It was just like her to walk off after speaking so vindictively.

Although this time I wasn't even sure if it was truth or lies. There was only one way that I was going to find out the whole truth, I wasn't a teenager hiding behind secretly hidden cameras anymore.

This time I would have to go directly to the parties involved, I was never good at confrontation, however this time it looked like it would be a requirement of my day.

My dad seemed to have anticipated my coming to him, as soon as he saw my face he suggested that we move to a private room to speak. Once alone in the room he offered me a drink.

"Would you like one?"

He asked, holding up a glass of fifty year old scotch, he only ever drank it at funerals or weddings usually.

"It's not my wedding day yet, Dad."

I said and refused the drink. Something told me that I wasn't going to like what he had to say. He continued on despite my tone.

"Not long now though. At least this time you are marrying a good one."

He replied. I'm sure he meant well but there was an angry fire in my belly that couldn't be quenched by polite conversation nor Scotch, no matter how aged it was.

I turned to face the man in front of me, a potential philanderer. Could he truly be the person Heather had accused him to be? They did talk on the phone a lot.

"Can you tell me, what is a 'good one'? You see I thought that the whole point of the wedding vows was to follow them, I especially like the bit about staying faithful. You must have missed that one, right? Or did your church give you different vows to follow? Does being related by law cause the wedding to go differently?"

I asked. My dad's smile faded as he looked into his empty glass, placing it down he grabbed the glass meant for me and swigged that down too.

The silence was painful for both of us. He was clearly shocked by the fact I knew this new information.

"It was a long time ago, we hit a rough patch. Ronnie was a comfort, I mistook that for love. I'm human after all. Your mother forgave me, why can't you?"

He said, confirming everything I had feared. I looked at him sternly in the face.

"Is that why you spend all your time separated from each other, I always thought it was Mum's love of the company that caused her to become distant from you. I even felt sorry for you, do you know that I wind her up regularly of how she cheats on you with our company. I call the company her toy boy on the side. When all the while you are the reason, behind all of it. You would have been kinder going through with the divorce, maybe then she would be happy now."

I shouted. William stared at me with hurt in his eyes, I had possibly gone too far yet I couldn't turn back now.

"We stayed together for you, we both agreed that our love for you was enough. I couldn't break your heart at ten years old, how could I?"

He replied. I saw the regret in his face as soon as he said the words out loud, clearly I wasn't supposed to know that either.

Chapter Twenty-Six

I couldn't believe it, they had been harbouring this secret for nearly twenty years.

"What happened to not keeping secrets from me ever again? Don't you remember what secrets did to this family in the first place?"

I replied. William tried to place his hand on my arm, like it was a knee jerk reaction I pulled away.

"You were just a kid Abby, I couldn't leave you behind."

He said. So not only were my parents both liars, but they still saw me as a helpless child.

"That was nearly twenty years ago, Dad!"

I screamed. I felt like I was losing my mind.

"I tried to tell you about it, I was saving it for your eighteenth birthday. But then you adopted Simon and had already been through so much. I didn't want to pile on."

He replied. My face fell.

"So what? If I'd stayed in America would you have finally divorced? If I'm what's holding you together then please break up. I'm a grown woman. I no longer need you to pretend to be happily married for my sake."

I said. My heart felt like it was breaking in two.

"It's not as simple as you're making it out to be, Abby. Not everything is quite so black and white. I made a commitment to your mother, I chose to stay with her. I have no reason to leave her side. I haven't heard from Ronnie in over twenty years, she disappeared out of my life as quickly as she entered it. If we're being honest, I went to meet her one night and she wasn't there. After I realised she wasn't coming back I saw what a fool I had been, I confessed everything to your mother and I nearly lost you both."

He said. I can't believe my mother would ever refuse to let me see my dad no matter what he had done wrong.

"I'm sorry to have disappointed you Abby, I should have told you. I will not apologise for sticking around to raise you. You are the greatest achievement of my life."

He continued.

"Dad, you haven't disappointed me. I'm certain Mum wouldn't have stopped you from being able to see your only daughter. I just wish you hadn't made life decisions to keep me happy which only served to make you both miserable."

I said. Trying hard to calm down. William went quiet.

"Look, I may not have told you everything. There are things about me I'm certain you wouldn't like."

William said. I leaned forward and squeezed him tightly.

"You're my one and only father, I was wrong to demand so much of you. You're human after all."

I said. Pulling away I smiled at him.

"I guess I know where I got my skills as a cheater from. Let's hope I don't end up cheating on Nicholas."

I said jokingly, but truly the thought had crossed my mind.

"You've been through hell and back Abby, you didn't cheat on Ralph because it's in your DNA. Trust me, it's not. You made a mistake but I see how much love you have for that new, soon to be, son in law of mine. You won't end up like your mother and I."

He said in reply. His confidence in me raised my spirits.

"Do you want to know any more secrets of the past or shall we nip this in the bud?"

My dad asked, his wide smile cheered me up.

"I've had as many secrets as I can take. Whatever else you got to tell me can't be as bad as this. Let's just forget I even know about the affair. You kept Thomas a secret from Mum, I can keep the fact I know about Ronnie a secret too."

I answered him. I decided to pour myself a large glass of scotch.

"You owe me this though."

I said before downing the glass. It was potent stuff but after that conversation I truly needed it.

Before my father had a chance to reply I left the room. Feeling a little light headed I bumped into my mother who had clearly come to check on us.

"Sorry Mother but don't worry, we are only human after all."

I said, before winking at my dad. I was feeling rather merry.

I headed straight to my cousin's bedroom, I could hear her schmoozing some clients on the phone. Bursting through the door unannounced she awkwardly excused herself from the phone conversation, promising to call them back.

Heather stared at me with annoyance oozing from her features.

"Are you out of your damn mind? That was an important business meeting!"

She shouted. I must admit it was nice to see that fake smile wiped off of her face.

"Oh, I'm sorry! Did it put a crimp in your day like maybe finding out your father was a cheat? Don't bullshit me saying that you thought I knew! You may have everyone else fooled, not me! I still see the same mean, stuck up skinny cow that I had to endure the presence of when growing up!"

I said. Heather's presence was starting to sober me up.

I had not purposely come in here to attack Heather, in fact I needed her help if anything but I was so infuriated by the situation I had found myself in. She was just a really easy target, I expected her to come back at me all guns blazing yet it was quite the opposite.

"Nice to know what you really think of me. Was I really that horrible to be around? I saw myself as your role model."

She said. I laughed a little thinking she was joking until I realised that she honestly believed what she was saying. I could see in her eyes that she was being genuine, it was a strangely warped version of reality in that head of hers. I attempted to backtrack, unsuccessfully.

"Um… yeah. Truthfully I always felt inadequate next to you. You weren't exactly nice to me."

I replied. Heather mulled over what I had said, for a brief moment I saw the real Heather just before her fake smile returned. Her face could easily be used as a mask in any emotional event.

"Well, we're big girls now. What is it you want? You can't have come here just to tell 'young me' off!"

She said. As much as I wanted to persevere with my mission to gain information about Ronnie, something held me back.

I'm not sure if it was that moment of innocence that I had witnessed, it had been brief but true. Perhaps the only genuine honest moment we had ever shared, I just had to know why she was the way she was.

I stared at her, my expression was one of confusion mixed up with sympathy.

"Why do you do that?"

I asked. Heather just grinned at me.

"Do what? Be fabulous, it just happens naturally."

She replied. Annoyance began to set in, however I shoved it back down, swallowing my pride along with it.

"That fake smile... you hide every real emotion with this pretend happiness and allure. You might have the rest of the world fooled Heather, I know you aren't happy. I can see that clearly now. So why fake it?"

I asked. Heather scoffed loudly at my words still adorned with that unbearable smirk.

"What did you expect? A good old heart to heart truth session? Did you want me to tell you how I envied you too, that I saw your family as perfection and I wanted to have your parents instead of my own? Do you want me to grovel on my knees for forgiveness for all my horrible behaviour as a teenager? Did you think that I have some sob story like being molested as a child to excuse who I have become? Nobody is happy Abigail, there are no happy endings. Marriage is about what you can get out of each other, before your looks fade. My parents never loved each other, they are as happily married as they come. Now if you will excuse me..."

Heather announced, she tried to leave but I blocked her path.

"Is that true? Any of what you just said? You didn't say it by accident, you are desperate for one real person to talk to. I recognise the pain in your eyes, I've seen it before in my own reflection. Who hurt you?"

I asked, feeling determined. She looked up at me as if she was about to shout but instead tears came out.

Ashamed of her own emotions she tried to hide her anguish.

"It's not easy being pretty you know! You might think that I had a great life. All the girls wanted to be me and all of the boys wanted to date me. The perfect breeding means a perfect life. Right?"

She asked through a flood of tears. I could have disagreed but this was my line of thinking.

"Well you're wrong! My parents detested each other, they hid it well and only showed their disdain for each other around me. I wasn't allowed to express any of my emotions. Do you think I actually want to marry well? No, I'd be happier with nobody. At least he wouldn't be sleeping with the temp in our copier room! I loved someone once, my parents didn't approve. So, of course I had to break his heart. I've had to do a lot of things that I didn't want to, my Mother practically forced me into sleeping my way to the top. I remember the first time that I had sex, he was the most popular boy in the school. The girls envied me, I basked in their awe as I became the first of our group to lose my virginity. Until the next day when I caught him fingering my best friend. She said it was only fair that I shared with her, a man like him could never be satisfied with one woman. So I turned a blind eye for the sake of appearances, I've been doing exactly that ever since. I'd love the luxury of marrying for love, I don't get the guy of my dreams... not like you. Perhaps seeing you so happy made me jealous, I did say that stuff about Ronnie to upset you."

She said. Her hurt was real whether I understood it or not. I wasn't sure what to say, instead I sat beside her on the bed and gave her a hug.

We must have sat there for over five minutes in silence.

"I think you should tell your parents how you feel. You will never be free until you do. It might be hard but you can always stay with me here. I went through a lot of horrible relationships before meeting the man I love. I'm certain you can find the man of your dreams too if you give it a real shot."

I said. She laughed curtly in reply.

"If I tell my parents any of this, I'll be cut off so I will definitely need a place to stay."

Heather said as she exhaled loudly before composing herself.

"I think you owe it to yourself to at least try and be happy."

I replied. Wiping away her tears she looked at me curiously.

"Why did you come here?"

She asked. I had nearly forgotten the very reason that I came here in the first place.

© This work is copyrighted

"I was hoping for information about Ronnie, I wanted to talk to her. I'm not sure why."

I said honestly. With the anger having dissipated I was left with an empty feeling, I still wanted to meet the 'other woman'. I just had no idea what to do after I did. I honestly had no idea what I had hoped to achieve.

"All I know is that her name was Veronica Baker, she met him in a bar when we were kids. I remember the argument between him and my mum. She was mad at him, she kept saying things like 'if you leave now than what was it all for?'. Or something like that."

Heather said. That was a start at least.

"So she lives in America then?"

I asked.

"I met her once, I snuck downstairs to grab a glass of milk. She was waiting for Uncle Bill. She said that she was just visiting and that William was going to join her in England soon. Of course I didn't know

about his affair, not until I saw them kissing in the car. Your dad begged me to keep it a secret. He told me that soon he was going to tell everyone, he said he loved her and was going to marry her. I truly didn't understand the whole thing way back then. Next thing I know Deidre and William are still together, Ronnie disappeared and I'm not even sure your mum even knew about her. Just tread carefully, your mum could be the reason that she disappeared."

She said. If that was true I would have to search for her incognito. I truly didn't know what my parents were capable of anymore.

In order for me to do that I would have to use my own means to discover the truth. I needed someone who wasn't on my parents pay roll.

"Can you teach me? How to bury my feelings and fake it? It might come in handy in my near future."

I asked. Heather laughed at me.

"Consider me your new teacher!"

She replied. Heather quickly sent a message on her phone, after she was done she showed me what she wrote.

It was to her fiancé, she had just dumped him. Heather had sent a picture of him and 'miss temp' on the copier both half naked. In case he tried to cause a problem for her, she had kept a lot of unflattering information on her conquests for that exact reason. She was a shrewd businesswoman if I ever did see one, I was quite proud to be her cousin in that moment.

Chapter Twenty-Seven

Heather decided to stay on at the manor, her parents were unaware of her recent break up. She was just waiting for my wedding to be over before she could let them know that she wasn't coming back to America with them.

I hadn't even told Nick about my dad's indiscretions, I didn't want to run the risk of ruining our wedding. Even Simon was entirely unaware of the secrets I was now keeping. I was completely ready to get married after making Heather my maid of honour.

Juliette couldn't make it to my wedding so there was an opening. I decided it would be a nice way to extend an olive branch to Heather. She looked stunning in her dress, a dress she chose herself. Knowing her like I do she wouldn't have had it any other way.

I clutched tightly to my dad's arm, I was nervous. Not only was I keeping a massive secret from all the people that I loved, I was about to become Mrs Romanos. This time it felt right, I had no doubt in my mind that Nicholas was the guy that I wanted to marry.

The ceremony was intimate, only close friends and family were present. We had fed the press a false location and date, just to ensure that we would get privacy. I exhaled one last time before the music began playing, the doors opened ready for my entrance.

Nicholas looked devastatingly handsome, as did Simon who stood beside him. I barely recognised him, he looked like a man. The little kid I once read bedtime stories to was now a grown up, I walked slowly towards them fighting back the tears.

As I reached my soon to be husband's side, my father's arm slipped away. I looked into Nicholas's eyes, I couldn't wait to spend the rest of my life with him. We spoke our vows out loud, both of us managed to stay tear free for the whole service.

I couldn't help but giggle nervously in places, my eyes would catch his and the shared smile would cause a glow to form inside of me. I just couldn't help but wonder if I should have shared my secret with my husband before we said our vows.

The rest of the day seemed to run in a fast forward motion, there were so many people giving me hugs and congratulations. I held Nicholas's hand all through the meal and toast, secretly I felt worried that I might wake up and it would all have just been a dream.

As long as I could feel his touch I knew it was really happening, his warm sensual embrace as we danced sent me to a place of euphoria. It felt as though there were no other people in that room apart from us, I never wanted that dance to end.

Sadly my parents felt the need to cut in, Nicholas danced merrily with my mum while I put on a brave face for my dad. It was getting harder and harder to fake it. I couldn't tell him I was looking for his ex nor could I discuss our private conversation in public.

Heather was always there reminding me to stay strong. If she could leave her rich fiancé I could fake it with my parents. When the party was in full swing I gave Heather my key so that she could go and sneak into my dad's office to see if she could find any clues.

She pretended to be suffering from severe menstrual cramps, a move I had used many years ago now. I made sure that my parents were liquored up and having a great time, even Heather's parents let loose on the dance floor.

Alcohol was the cure for most people's social issues, I made a point of staying sober. I even managed to catch Simon alone, he was waiting for Anya to come back from the bathroom so I made the most of it.

"Hey kiddo! Having fun?"

I asked. Simon smiled.

"Of course, congrats. You happy?"

He replied. I nodded.

"Very. Are you? You have been distant lately. I was worried you might not be entirely happy for me."

I said. Simon looked concerned.

"No, nothing like that. I have just been giving you space. I don't wanna get in the way of you two, he really loves you. He's a good guy."

He said. I grabbed Simon, squeezing him briefly.

"I will never need space from you. I miss you. We haven't had any 'us' time in forever."

I said. Simon laughed at me, clearly me missing my son was funny to him.

"Let's have breakfast, soon."

I pleaded with him..

"Sure, I'd like that. You look beautiful Mum."

He replied. With that last moment Anya returned, I left them to get back on the dance floor. My only interest now was in getting out of here, with my new husband.

We waved goodbye to our adoring fans, Nicholas had booked us the best room in our favourite hotel.

"You look stunning Mrs Romanos."

Nicholas said as he looked at me adoringly.

"You don't look too bad yourself, Dr Romanos."

I said as I kissed his luscious lips, they looked good enough to eat.

He unzipped my heavy wedding dress as we began disrobing, we hadn't been intimate in over a week. The wedding plans had overtaken our lives, finally it was all over. He was all mine, forever.

Nicholas stood before me in the nude, he caressed my breast as I stroked his stiff member. I had no intention of waiting any longer, I needed him inside of me now. I pushed him gently onto our large king size bed, climbing on top of him eagerly I slipped his penis inside of me.

I began rolling around on top of him, up and down, back and forth. I could feel his need for release, I teased him as he played with my nipples. He had enough of waiting for me, as soon as he felt my orgasm had reached completion he was eager to start his.

He pressed himself deep inside of me, after a few strokes up and down he began going harder. He clung to me tightly as he lay on top of me groaning, he began to slow down after he was able to cum.

We lay there sweaty and lifeless, I didn't want to free his limp penis just yet. I began moving back and forward ever so gently until I could feel him harden inside of me again, he flipped me over as he thrust behind me.

Gently he caressed my clitorous in time with his movements, it sent me wild as I felt out of control. Ecstasy took over me as I moaned in pleasure, he made sure that we both came at the same time. I had never felt so at ease with my sexuality than in that moment, we were man and wife enjoying the pleasure of each other's bodies. It was beautiful, sensual, just perfect.

Chapter Twenty-Eight

I slept peacefully on my wedding night, the amazing sex was probably the main reason. However, knowing that the stress of planning my wedding was now officially over meant I could relax.

My relaxation didn't last long, my phone woke me up from my slumber. Heather had been able to locate the information that I needed. Although now I had to confide in my husband in order to avoid the secret becoming a problem.

"Nicholas, are you awake?

I whispered. He began to stir.

"I am now."

He replied sounding rather sleepy. The twinkle in his eye would suggest he misunderstood why I'd woken him up.

"I have to tell you something."

I said. Nicholas grew sullen as he sat up in bed beside me.

"Nothing bad I hope."

He replied. There could be any number of things going through his head right now. I decided to just spit it out so that he could stop worrying.

"I wasn't able to tell you this before but my father had an affair when I was ten. I didn't want to put you in a position where you had to keep a secret from your new in-laws right before we said 'I do'. Except I feel I have to tell you now because I've

been trying to find a way to track down his mistress."

I replied. Nicholas looked a little confused.

"Why do I feel like there is a 'but' coming?"

He said. I smiled a little before revealing what that 'but' was.

"I can't use any of my family's resources to find her as I'm not willing to tell my parents what I'm up to. I'm not certain I can trust them, they have kept a lot of secrets from me and were very good at it. I need to know the truth about the affair and why she disappeared off of the face of the planet so suddenly."

I continued. Nicholas's concern grew.

"I get the feeling that your parents aren't to be trifled with. I may have a way to help you but I need to know if you've truly considered the consequences of unearthing secrets that may be better off buried."

He said. I knew he was right but I couldn't live my life feeling the way I was right now.

"I need to know the answers, I'm willing to deal with what comes next. It's not the first time I've been responsible for revealing a huge family secret."

I said. Nicholas raised one eyebrow.

"That doesn't put my mind at ease, the fallout from that caused you years of pain."

He replied. I kissed his cheek gently causing his worry to lessen.

"I won't confront my parents unless I have to, this is mostly for my own peace of mind. It won't be like before. I promise."

I reassured him. Nicholas sighed before letting me in on a secret of his own.

"I have a private detective I trust with my life, he is the one who helped Sonia and I with our divorces. He has strict rules but he can get any information on anyone."

He revealed. I grabbed him excitedly. After squeezing the life out of him I gave him a big kiss on the lips.

Sadly we couldn't hang around too long in bed as we both had to get back to reality. We had both agreed that Cyprus was going to be our honorary honey moon as neither of us could afford time off right now.

I was happy that Nicholas was now on my side and had a means of getting the information on Veronica Baker. I just had to meet up with Heather in private in order to get what I needed to begin the search.

We apparently missed a lot of drama, Heather's parents had left her behind after a massive row. I was proud of her for finally sticking up for herself. I asked Nicholas to keep my parents busy while I pretended to be checking up on her.

At first I was worried Nicholas wouldn't be comfortable playing defence for me but he was perfectly comfortable schmoozing my parents so I could slip away. I didn't want to draw too much attention to my newfound friendship with my previously hated cousin.

I found Heather sitting alone in the green room.

"Hey, I heard it didn't go very well."

I said. She had been sitting by a small lamp, the lighting in the room was dim. As I sat besides her I noticed that she was flicking through an old family photo album.

"I can't believe how young we were."

She said. Heather sounded nostalgic. I could see a recognisable picture of us at her parents lake-house. We had to be only about nine years old.

"I barely remember this, we look like good friends here. It wasn't long before we became frenemies."

I said before placing my open palm onto her back before continuing.

"By the looks of that photo we were having a good time, I'm not actually sure what happened to us."

I replied honestly, I couldn't remember a good with Heather. Yet right in front of me was evidence to the contrary.

We were in the middle of a water gun fight giggling, happier than I had ever remembered being. Most of my memories were of our disagreements.

"Sometimes the bad is easier to remember than the good. Take me and Matthew for example, I know we had good times. I just can't remember any of them. All I remember was the viscously cruel things that he did to me. Remembering any good just felt like it had to be a lie."

I tried to rationally explain it away, I should be able to remember more than the bad blood between my cousin and I. Heather attempted a smile.

"Sounds just like the description of my childhood, not that there was any physical abuse. If anything it was all psychological, nothing I could ever do would ever be good enough for my Mother. She wasn't ever satisfied with my abilities, she would just tell me that I could do better. Any grade I got wasn't as good as she got, any job I managed to get into wasn't well paid enough. I would constantly be reminded of who I was, who my grandfather was. You have the same grandfather, yet you got to live life freely. Your parents never forced you to be 'great'."

She replied. Heather stood up placing the pictures back where they were originally.

"I may not have been treated badly because of my grandfather but my grandma sure did a number on me."

I replied. Heather nodded sympathetically. It was clear we had both been through a lot. I stayed with her until Nicholas came to find me. She was in no fit state to be left alone.

Chapter Twenty-Nine

Nicholas had decided to take our bags back to our room considering the state we found Heather in.

I was a little out of my depth, Heather and I hadn't been close for as long as I can remember. I sat thinking for a moment.

"Is that why you started lashing out at me? Because of the secret you had to keep for my dad? Or was it just because of how your parents treated you?"

I asked.

"I guess it was a bit of both, resentment for you built up into envy and hatred. I can't say that I was in control, it was just an outlet. Something just switched inside of me."

She replied. I smiled at my cousin knowingly.

"I can't say my life was perfect, but I had it good. Until I came to live here that is. I had a chance to go back, now I wonder if I should have taken it."

I replied feeling pensive. Unexpectedly Heather reached over to squeeze my hand, I guess we had more in common than I thought. We had spent so long being rivals, we could have been allies this whole time.

I left Heather alone after she gave me the file on Veronica Baker, she clearly had a lot to think about. Nicholas had managed to pack all of our stuff away by the time I got back upstairs.

"Is your cousin alright?"

He asked. I nodded as I lay my body down onto our bed.

"She will be, I never knew her life was so challenging. I thought she had it easy, it goes to show how little we know about people really."

I replied before turning my attention back to my husband, as I looked him up and down I couldn't help but smile at him.

"Speaking of which, I never knew my husband could lie so well. You practically charmed the pants off of my parents back there."

I said. Nicholas laughed wholeheartedly at my mockery.

"I clearly have hidden talents."

He replied as he leaned in to give me a kiss but I pulled back just an inch so that I could look him in the eyes.

"Seriously though, I shouldn't be worried... Should I?"

I asked. Nicholas furrowed his brow before pecking my lips, pulling back he looked me dead in my eyes.

"Just because I can lie, doesn't mean I will ever lie to you. I will save my superpower for our enemies."

He said whilst winking briefly, he was clearly joking with me.

"Seriously though, I love you. Secrets and lies destroy relationships, I don't want that for us. That was why I didn't get upset at the fact you didn't tell me about your parents' affair, you had your reasons to delay telling me. I am just happy that you did tell me. I trust you fully, I hope you trust me too."

Nicholas said. He had a good point, he'd never given me any reason to doubt him. Content with his answer I embellished in a real kiss, it felt good to be married.

As much as I wanted to focus on all the good in my life, I couldn't get Veronica Baker out of my mind. Once Nicholas had settled down to sleep I grabbed the file Heather had given me.

There really wasn't much here but at least I now had a photo of her and some photocopies of the emails sent to my father. He'd kept them all this time, it was clear to me that my father was still harbouring feelings for Ronnie.

I planned to make contact tomorrow with Nicks's P.I. yet I couldn't help myself. I called him up and he gave me details of where to meet him. With my husband taking a much needed nap I decided to go meet him alone.

We met in an isolated location, he insisted on only knowing each other by face only. No names or personal details were given on either side. I handed him the file and I was told not to get in touch. I saved him on my phone as Mr Nobody.

If and when he found out anything he would let me know. Until then I had to sit tight, something I admittedly wasn't very good at. By the time I reached home Nicholas was wide awake.

"There you are Abby, Nicholas has been looking for you. Apparently you switched your phone off and didn't let him know you were popping out."

Deidre announced.

"Ah yes, just popped out for a bit but forgot to charge my phone. Where is he now?"

I asked, trying to act casual. She pointed behind me, Nicholas must have heard my voice.

"There you are, I just got a call from my mum. My dad has had a heart attack. I need to fly out to see him."

He said looking worried.

"I'll come with you."

I replied instantly then turned around to see if my mother approved. After a small nod of her head I turned back around to look at Nicholas.

"Ok, I'll book us a flight…"

He started to say.

"Take the jet, it'll be faster. I'll tell the pilot to get ready, you just go pack your things."

My mother said as she interrupted him.

We did as we were told and hurriedly said goodbye before boarding the private jet. I wasn't sure how to broach the subject of my meeting with his private detective and wasn't sure now was even the time, so I decided to wait until an opportune moment to bring it up.

Nicholas was on edge for the whole flight, I tried hard to reassure him that everything was going to be ok, but even I thought it sounded hollow.

"It isn't the first time he's had problems with his heart. That's why I've been trying to convince them to come live with us. It's part of the reason why I wanted a big house."

He said. I actually had no idea he was planning for his parents to live with us.

"I'm all for it, but you know better than anyone how stubborn your parents can be about these things."

I said, trying to be gentle with him. He agreed but was clearly feeling emotional so I left him alone after that. It was a quiet flight but thankfully a quick one.

Chapter Thirty

Our trip to Cyprus had been an emotional one, his father had been in critical condition when we arrived. Thankfully Nicholas was able to swoop in and save the day. I left him there as he decided to stay behind and try hard to convince his parents to come home with him.

I had to get back home so I took the jet and flew back to the manor. A week later Nicholas also returned but unfortunately his parents had refused to come back with him.

Nicholas had already sold his house and he had found one he had liked. He was keen on showing me our potential new home but insisted that Simon be present too. I managed to convince Simon it would not be boring viewing houses as he would have me for company.

We reached our destination and Nicholas was looking extremely proud of him as he showed us around. Once the tour was done he asked us what we thought. Simon looked very impressed.

"It's stunning Nicholas."

I replied. Nicholas looked like a little kid at Christmas.

"It's ours, I bought it."

He announced. I was a little shocked to hear it was already a done deal but nevertheless I adored the place.

"I love it."

I said. Nicholas grabbed me and span me around. I looked at him feeling concerned.

"I'm going to quit my job. I want to find a job that I enjoy doing. If I quit can we still live here?"

I asked. Nicholas smiled in reply.

"I was actually hoping you were going to say that, I have been offered a local job. More correctly I have put in my resume and they called me to offer a job. The hospital around here is smaller but they want me to run it, it means that I will be local and earn more money. My hours shouldn't change from what I do now, I was thinking that you could take the time off of work to do some university courses from home. Anything you like, I want you to have a job that you love. What do you think?"

He replied. I had never truly thought about doing that, yet as he said it out loud I knew deep down that was exactly what I had always wanted to do.

"What do you think, Simon? Could you live here with us?"

I asked. Simon smiled, pulling us in for a squeeze.

"Like one big happy family!"

He teased as he placed his head between ours, releasing us shortly after.

"Now I just have to break the news to your grandparents that not only are we moving out but I'm leaving the family business too."

I said feeling nervous.

"Yeah, I'm not going to help you with that. I'll help Nick with moving our stuff instead."

Simon said. Agreeing to his plan of action I left the men in my life to sort out our moving plans while I texted my father, asking that we could speak.

He was in his office just as he usually was, I pulled out his favourite whiskey and placed it down alongside two glasses.

"What's the occasion?"

He asked.

"I'm giving you your freedom."

I replied. He looked at me feeling confused.

"Nicholas, Simon and I are moving out. I am also going to be leaving the company."

I continued. William quickly poured himself a drink and swigged it down.

"Is this because of the affair?"

He asked.

"No Dad, it's just time for me to live my life separately to you guys."

I said. He poured himself another drink and nursed it in his hand.

"What about Cliff? What about your Mum? She can't run that company alone."

He asked.

"Cliff will hopefully not know where I live and finally leave us all alone. As for Mum, well she has Grace. That girl does my job better than me by far."

I replied. I poured myself a glass and raised it, offering him a toast.

"You've lived your life to please others for too long, it's time you lived the way you want to."

I said. He clinked my glass and we both drank our drinks.

"You are my life Abby, can you at least promise to let us visit."

He said. I leant over and gave him a kiss on his cheek.

"Mi casa es su casa, Dad. You will always be welcome."

I replied. I left him alone with his thoughts while I went to go find my mother. I doubt my conversation with her would go quite as well.

Chapter Thirty-One

It had been a rough month, so much had transpired in such a small space of time. I quit my job, moved out of the manor. My mother was still very angry with me abandoning her. Our conversation ended up in a row and she hadn't spoken to me since.

The private detective had only contacted me to let me know he had hit a dead end so was working on a different angle. I was beginning to think the worst over where she might be.

I convinced my dad to buy me out of my piece of the manor. I'd severed all ties between my charity's so that the estate could be out from under me. I took a step back from my charity work so that I could be less involved wherever possible.

Zuzanna was happy to accommodate me so long as I stayed involved in the charity in one way or another. I agreed to still be a part of her charities as well as mine, but just for public appearance purposes. I was finally free from my grandma's inheritance and my family's legacy, it was like I had just unshackled myself from chains that had been keeping me in a prison cell.

The adoption agency were more than satisfied with our new accommodations, we had been officially put on the waiting list. We didn't want to wait around for a baby, we were hoping for an older child.

Perhaps one who really needed a home, just as Simon did all those years ago. Heather had also moved in with us, hopefully it would just be a temporary arrangement. I liked her now but she had been a little mopey lately.

I was responsible for her being homeless after all, she had been applying for newspaper jobs all over the country, however she was still waiting on replies. So it looked like for the meantime we had a pretty full house, thankfully our house was big enough for them all to fit comfortably.

I was busy looking at jobs in the local area when I heard my phone chime. The private detective finally had something for me. After confessing to Nicholas a few weeks ago that I'd been in touch he had decided that he wanted to stay out of it.

As much as he loved me he didn't want to get involved in my determination to dig up the past. So considering he wasn't going to come with me I decided to take Heather out of the house.

Heather came with me but refused to come out of the car. I hurried to meet up with the P.I. before rushing back to show Heather the information he had gathered.

"That can't be accurate."

Heather said. I looked at her with the same worried expression.

"Ronnie, she's Cliff's niece. That can't be a coincidence."

I announced. Heather grabbed the file and looked at it closely.

It turns out that Veronica was Cliff's twin's child, he had her last known address and proof that she used to go by a different surname. The thing that bothered me was the fact she had a daughter aged twenty-one which would mean she could have been pregnant around about the time she disappeared.

What's worse is that she had named her daughter Grace, I had no proof yet but what if the Grace I knew was the same Grace that was in this file.

"Mum might be in trouble."

I said. Heather looked confused but there was no time to explain. I rang my mum's number but she wasn't the one to answer the call.

"Why Abigail, just the girl I wanted to hear from."

The sinister voice seeped through my end of the phone, the look of horror alerted Heather to my discomfort.

I put the phone on the loud speaker as I mouthed the words 'It's Cliff'.

"What do you want Cliff? How did you get my mother's phone?"

I asked. My phone alerted me to an incoming video call, I answered revealing an image of my parents tied up in the function room.

He flipped the camera back around to his crude and evil looking features, he was wearing some kind of explosive vest. Just like the one Max had worn.

My parents looked terrified.

"If you don't come here and convince your parents to sign over all they have to me, well let's just say there will be one more firework display happening right here in your beloved home. Your parents will volunteer to be the Catherine wheels, of course. You have one hour to arrive here with documents drafted up ready to be signed over to me. Involve the police and your parents are dead."

He said. I had no idea how he managed to pull this one off, if it was the last thing I was going to do I was going to stop him.

Chapter Thirty-Two

I looked at Heather feeling desperate.

"What am I going to do?"

I asked. Heather of course did not have an answer to my question. I raced back home. I had to come up with a plan quickly. I grabbed Nicholas and told Heather to stay with Simon. They were under strict instructions to stay here where it was safe.

I had no clue how to get my family out of this.

"I hate to admit it but we need help, I was thinking…"

I started saying. It was as if Nicholas could sense what I was about to say.

"Oh no! We are not going to ask for help from your psycho ex!"

He replied.

"Why can't you call the police?"

Nicholas insisted.

"Every time I involve the police, Cliff gets away! This is no joke, my parents' lives are on the line. We need to go see Thomas."

I said. Thomas was highly trained, despite his ridiculous melt down I had heard that he was doing better.

He was the only person I knew that had a chance of helping us in this situation. Without the ability of involving the police, my options were limited. The mansion was under threat, I had to do everything in my power to stop him.

"Nicholas, please... What other choice do we have?"

Nicholas exhaled loudly.

"I really don't like the guy Abby, Thomas shot you! Or have you forgotten about that part?"

He asked angrily. I hadn't, I still carried the scar from the injury.

I sat down in front of him, I hoped that if I gave him a few minutes he would begin to realise that I was right. Nicholas got up and began pacing.

"The only way I will be willing to let him help you is if I come too, non negotiable."

He replied. The last thing I wanted was to put Nicholas in danger.

"Only if you agree to let me go in alone, I'm not risking your life as well as mine. Besides we don't want to spook Cliff. He needs to think he's won."

I replied. He agreed to my terms despite clearly not wanting to. We headed off to talk to Thomas, he was living not far from here by himself.

After some time doing community service he was released and now worked at a local bar, having been disgraced he was no longer welcome in the fire service. We were now sitting in the car outside of his apartment.

"I am so sorry you have to do this Nicholas, I honestly think it is our only shot. He knows all about bombs, weapons and strategies for attack and rescue. Before he became a firefighter he served his country."

I said. Nicholas pulled me in for a kiss.

"I would do absolutely anything for you, even if it includes hanging out with your crazy ex while we take down your son's evil grandfather."

He replied. I laughed a little but what we were about to do weighed heavily on me.

"I'm gonna need you to call your assistant up, she's going to draft us some fake paperwork."

I said. Nicholas called her quickly to explain what we needed her to do. There was really no way that I could reassure myself or Nicholas that this would be worth our time, let alone that even with his help it might all be futile anyway.

Chapter Thirty-Three

As I knocked on the door, worry and fear filled inside of me like a wave of destruction.

"Who is it?"

Chimed loudly through the PVC door.

"Abigail."

I replied. He opened the door widely, first he looked at me in shock then he noticed Nicholas standing beside me.

"I don't want any trouble. I have done my time for my crimes against you."

He said. Thomas looked a little scared as he hovered in the open doorway.

"As much as I would like to punch you in your face for shooting Abby, Thomas. That is not why we are here. Are you going to let us in?"

Nicholas said. Thomas hesitated at first but eventually he let us in.

His place of residence wasn't exactly inviting, it was a little unkempt and looked like he slept on the sofa last night. The couch had an unwashed blanket draped across it, the whole of the ground around it was surrounded by a minefield of empty beer cans.

We decided to stay standing.

"Sorry, my cleaning lady is on holiday. So what brings you to my humble palace?"

Sarcasm dripped from the mouth of a very annoyed Thomas. We were clearly not welcome here.

"We need your help. Cliff has my parents, he is wearing a bomb vest and threatening to blow up the mansion. You are the only guy I know who isn't police or police adjacent that knows about bombs."

I said. Thomas looked at us both for a moment.

"I do owe you one and it isn't like I have anything better to do. I guess, I'm in."

He said. I was surprised at the quick turnaround, not that I was complaining.

"What about Mr Tough guy over there, is he gonna let me live when we spend time alone?"

He asked. I looked at Nicholas's stern expression before allowing him to answer Thomas's question.

"If I didn't come to kill you by now Thomas, after everything you have done to me; I guess I am not going to, alright?"

Nicholas replied. He spoke through gritted teeth but it was enough to stave his concerns.

After waiting in the car for about five minutes Thomas arrived, he was laden with heavy bags full of useful tools and weapons. After we had driven to a nearby safe house that my family had for emergencies we could finally talk.

"So, tell me Abigail. What is the situation?"

He asked. I showed Thomas the screen capture that I managed to get while having the video chat.

"Okay, I recognise the type of vest he is wearing. He is also holding the trigger in his hand, if we get him away from the trigger then the bomb can't go off."

He said. I wasn't so sure that would be a good option.

"What other options do we have, I don't think that Cliff is going to let go of that trigger considering it is his only bargaining chip."

I replied. Thomas went off to look through his bags.

Nicholas pulled me aside.

"Are you sure that we can't get the police involved?"

He asked. I shook my head.

"You know we can't baby, please bear with me. Did you get your assistant to fax over the fake paperwork to sign?"

Nicholas nodded, he quickly went over to a computer in Thomas's house to print them off.

"Okay, guys. This is going to be a three person job, but I may have another way to disarm the bomb. It would only be temporary, just long enough to get your parents out. I can try to get the trigger away

from him at this time but if I fail we all need to get out of the blast radius."

He said, holding up a device for us to look at. As he explained what it did I knew why it needed three people, one person needed to activate it using a laptop when it is within a metre of the device.

Someone would have to get the device a metre away and another would have to create a distraction, considering his training Thomas was best being unrestricted. Nicholas was going to stay with the laptop in our car, Thomas will be the one to tackle him once the device was disarmed, the device only worked for about a ten minute window.

I would have to go in with the paperwork, distract him long enough to let Thomas get into position. I could easily get within a metre of him considering I was there to sign fake paperwork with him, he was clearly not aware that I had signed over everything to my parents.

If he had become aware then my parents would have been in big trouble by now.

"Okay, so I am supposed to stay out with a laptop while Mr. Trigger happy gets to save the day."

Nicholas muttered under his breath. Thomas puffed out his chest in defence to Nicholas's complaints.

"Nicholas, he is putting himself in a lot of danger here. If he can't get away from Cliff within ten minutes and he presses the trigger then he could die. I need you to live."

I said. Backing down Nicholas agreed to go ahead with the plan.

"None taken, Kitten."

Thomas said. His smug smirk was unbearable.

"You owe me, your drunk shooting could have killed me. I don't mind you risking your life."

I replied. His smirk quickly faded.

Thomas and Nicholas drove up to a section of trees where they could stay hidden, they dropped him by the gate so that it would seem like I came alone. Once they were in position they would tell me through the hidden ear devices we were wearing.

"Be careful, please Abby."

Nicholas said. I leant in to give him a kiss, leaving the guys behind in the car.

I hoped that they could be left alone without fighting to their death. Holding the papers in my hand, I quickly placed the bomb deactivation device hidden inside of my bra. It was the only place to conceal it where he wouldn't notice it.

I rang my own doorbell, or at least my old home's doorbell. I waited for a minute, Cliff was the one to answer in his bomb vest trigger in hand just like in the video chat.

"Get inside!"

He snarled. Cliff grabbed my arm, hauling me through the door.

"I'm here now, you can let the staff go."

I said bravely. I could only assume he had them tied up somewhere. There was no sign of them anywhere. Ignoring me he shoved me into the green room.

My parents were still tied up in the same manner, I tried running to them but he would not let go of my arm.

"You have the documents?"

He asked. I handed the paperwork over and ran over to my parents.

"Are you guys okay?"

I asked before taking off their gags allowing them to speak.

"We're fine hunny, why did you come?"

My mum asked. I looked at my mum like she was crazy.

"How could I leave you? No matter what has gone on between us you are still my parents and I love you!"

I replied. Their expression turned to fear as I heard footsteps coming up from behind me.

"That is quite enough Miss Abigail, your signature is required first."

Cliff said as he pulled me away from my parents.

I quickly whispered the code word for the others to know I was going to start making a move, Thomas should be in position soon enough and ten minutes would have to be enough time for us to escape. I just had to keep Cliff distracted long enough for Thomas to let us know he had him in his sights.

Chapter Thirty-Four

I stood up slowly with my hands in the air.

"Okay Cliff, just so you know…"

I said, stepping a little closer to him, he had the trigger in his hand ready to press.

"…my signature is of no use to you, not only are those fake documents…"

I continued. I came one more step closer as he looked at me in disbelief.

"...I no longer own the estate you're standing on nor do I have any rights to sign over my parents company to you."

I said. Cliff looked angrily at me.

"You're a liar, even if that was the case I still have your parents! If you can't give me what I want, what is stopping me from blowing us all up to sky high?"

He asked. I heard Thomas speak quietly in my ear piece.

"Give me two more minutes, Kitten, I nearly have him in my sights"

He said. I thought about how I could distract him from pressing the trigger.

I stopped moving in so that Cliff would feel more at ease.

"Don't you have any reason to stay alive? What about your grandson that you tried to kidnap before? Or was that all just to get what doesn't belong to you?"

I asked. Antagonising him seemed to work.

"I don't care about that mongrel child of my idiot son! Everything I do is to hurt you and get what's rightfully mine. For your information it does belong to me! I gave your grandfather the idea that started his whole business! He owes me EVERYTHING!"

Cliff shouted. He began coughing severely, as he held a blood soaked tissue to his mouth I knew he must be dying.

"How long have you had lung cancer?"

I asked. Grandma Jean had faked her cancer so easily that I had taken time to learn all about the different types. Cliff looked up at me looking dishevelled.

"How did you know that I have lung cancer?"

He asked. I gestured towards the blood on his tissue, pulling it out of sight as he composed himself.

Looking across at my parents than at me he stood tall.

"I'm dying, I have weeks to live. I want to die with the estate in my name, once you sign the documents I will blow us all to sky high. If i can't have it none of us can. If it is in my name when you die than your descendants can't have it either. Now you have two choices Mr and Mrs Wilson, you can sign the deed or watch your only child die a horrible death."

He said. Thomas was finally ready, he gave us the sixty second countdown for Nicholas to press the button disabling the bomb remotely.

"Okay, Cliff. Let me just untie my parents. We will comply with your request."

I said. Turning around I winked at my parents, untying them now would save me time once the ten minutes had begun.

"Where is all the staff?"

I whispered.

"We have no staff anymore Abby."

My dad replied. Refusing to let my confusion over their reply get the better of me, I pressed on.

"Okay, what about Aunty C?"

I asked.

"She flew back home yesterday."

My mum replied. I seemed to have missed a lot but to be fair I too had a lot to catch them up on too.

Feeling confused I knew there was no time to waste. I was able to get my parents free before the sixty seconds were up, the first second that I knew it was a hundred percent disabled I made a move. Grabbing my parents we made a run for it.

"Stop!"

Cliff shouted. I turned around just long enough to see him press the trigger, nothing happened however Thomas grabbed a hold of him knocking him to the ground.

They were wrestling each other when I left them. Normally Thomas could have beaten Cliff quickly but he was out of shape and Cliff had nothing left to lose. I was worried he wouldn't make it out in time.

I managed to get my parents safely to Nicholas. It took us five minutes to get safely to the car. I waited, Cliff might have been old and dying but he was not an easy man to get the better of.

We heard a gunshot, I looked at Nicholas feeling even more concerned.

"Don't worry, he'll make it out."

Nicholas said, he was trying to reassure me. The ten minute window was up, I was about to start running towards the house when a massive explosion could be heard. I turned around to face the house and saw that the entire midsection was in flames.

I pointed to the house and looked at Nicholas.

"Thomas... he didn't come out!"

I shouted. Nicholas looked on in disbelief.

"Thomas! Thomas can you hear me?"

I spoke into the comms but there was no response. My parents hugged me tightly as I feared for the worst. What had I done? I should have gone to the police. Could Thomas really be gone?

To Be Continued...

Printed in Great Britain
by Amazon

85366320R00195